LEGEND OF THE SCYTHE

VOLUME – IV THE RETURN OF HAYADA

KARTIK JOSYULA

Legend of the Scythe

Copyright © 2025 by Kartik Josyula.

MILTON & HUGO L.L.C.
4407 Park Ave., Suite 5
Union City, NJ 07087, USA

Website: *www. miltonandhugo.com*
Hotline: *1- 888-778-0033*
Email: *info@miltonandhugo.com*

Ordering Information:
Quantity sales. Special discounts are granted to corporations, associations, and other organizations. For more information on these discounts, please reach out to the publisher using the contact information provided above.

Library of Congress Control Number: 2025902903
ISBN-13:   979-8-89285-482-5   [Paperback Edition]
              979-8-89285-483-2   [Hardback Edition]
              979-8-89285-484-9   [Digital Edition]

Rev. date: 02/12/2025

CONTENTS

DEDICATION

To Sita Lakshmi and Chandrasekhara Sastry, without whom
I may not have dared to dream. This work and all that follow
are the trees that grew from the seeds you've sown.

Song of Illusion

The final battle of the war between Daryudan's forces and humanity came to an end. As the remainder of the dark army scattered for their lives, the human forces rejoiced. Rejoiced, for there would be no more oppression, no more fear of annihilation, no more worry about the future of their children and their children. The demon, the immortal warlord Daryudan, had breathed his last and the warriors of light, through struggle and tribulation, brought forth the victory that was fabled in a prophecy two decades ago.

Daryudan's lifeless body was raised on to an altar made of swords and shields for all to see. A death befitting a warlord, for all the bad he wreaked upon the world, all the ill will and hatred he garnered and all the lives he took, the loss of his life would be celebrated for three whole days before he was allowed to burn and descend into the netherworld.

Layana and Merata were flocked by adoring soldiers, chants of their praise rang true and loud for hours on end. The kitchens of Laira sprang to life cooking up a storm of a feast for the human forces. The inns and taverns of Laira brought their finest mead and whoever was not injured helped set up tables and chairs for the feast to come.

Merata's eyes looked for Kyano. She hadn't seen him since the end of the battle. Weary from her own injuries, she beckoned a soldier that was close by, "Have you seen the prince?" she asked, her voice somber, yet insistent.

The soldier looked around as though he had just laid eyes on Kyano.

"No, my lady," he replied, "I shall seek him out for you," he added.

Merata's legs began to feel the weight of the battle upon her body, and she sank to the ground, resting her back against a wall. Taking deep breaths, she calmed herself and focused on healing. Her white energy came forth and covered her head to toe and she could feel every injury. She could feel every small cut and laceration that needed attention. Knowing that she did not have the strength or energy left to heal everything, she focused on the injuries around her ribs and stomach which seemed to be causing her the most amount of pain.

The soldier came back, a look of panic on his face. "We found the prince my lady," he said, "but he is not moving."

"What do you mean he is not moving?" Merata asked, not making any effort to hide the frustration in her voice, "Is he alright?"

"He is not breathing," replied the terrified infantryman.

"Take me to him now!" yelled Merata with as much strength as she could muster. Still reeling from her own injuries, she made her way through the troves of soldiers laughing and chanting Laira's praise.

On the west side of Laira's gate, by a destroyed guard tower lay the prince of Serin, unmoving, eyes closed.

Merata crashed to her knees by his side. She checked for a pulse, put her ear to his chest to hear his beating heart, put her fingers by his nose to sense the movement of air in and out of his lungs but to no avail. The Kyano that lay in front her was not breathing, his heart had stopped. He was, for all intents and purposes dead.

Shivering with panic, Merata summoned all of her energy and poured it into his heart to make it move again. Screaming at the top of her voice, she said, "Don't be dead, please, don't be dead!"

She felt her energy course through him and back into her. She put her hands together and thumped his chest repeatedly, barely able to see where she was pounding out of her tear-filled eyes. No matter what she did, he was not coming back.

As the reality of Kyano's death began to sink in, Merata picked up his head and put it on her lap. She stroked his hair as she cried. The celebration of victory over Daryudan suddenly became a bittersweet reality for all Lairans. The screams of joy turned into deafening silence. The festivities merged with disbelief.

Layana stood above Merata and stared at the corpse of her brother. She did her best to subdue her own rage at what she was witnessing as she looked, for signs of what killed the warrior who slayed demons. She knelt slowly, making absolutely certain not to avert her gaze from Kyano. She grasped Merata's shoulder and pulled her back a little. A surprised Merata looked at the princess, still in disbelief as tears poured out of her eyes. Layana, all the while still examining her brother's body had only one thing to say, "This thing is not him."

PREFACE

Part One: Child of Darkness

"Do you believe in purpose?" asked the child. Sitting on the edge of the wall, peering into the great darkness of night, "Do you really think there is a reason why anything happens or is it all just a farce?"

Dimarius was taken aback. Gods often showed higher intellect for their age. Age, a term loosely used by beings who existed outside the boundaries of time. Even though they had birth, and they grew to adulthood, there was no natural end to gods. They simply existed.

"Perhaps you should find your own purpose," replied the king of Gods, "Every God did the same. We choose what we want to do and how to do it my dear. Our purpose is an instrument of the circle of time. We all have a role to play in the grand scheme but what that role exactly is, well you will have to deduce that for yourself. Once you know what your powers are, you will have to make the great choice of how you will use them to aid creation."

"I already know what I can do father," she said, "I can make things happen. I can change anything about anyone. Make them think whatever I want them to."

Dimarius paused, his expression somber. He did not quite understand the extent of power this little god child had or would develop as she grew up. All he could gather at the time was that her power was dangerous, potentially even limitless.

"So can you make my beard black again?" he asked, doing his best to disguise his concern with amusement.

"I cannot change you, you are a god," snickered the little girl, "I can change what is real. When I do that, everybody forgets what once happened and will only know what I changed it to."

"Oh, is that so?" said Dimarius, looking impressed, "Have you done it before?"

"Only once," whispered the girl, "I made a boy think he was a bird, and he tried so hard to fly haha."

Now, he was sure. This power was dangerous and if not controlled, it could destroy all of existence. This little girl would grow up to be the most powerful God in all of time for she held authority over reality itself. He imagined her perspective for a moment, pondered over what it would be like to know what was and change what is so that the future was whatever he pleased it to be. For a God who could create worlds and fill them with life, even he felt powerless before her.

"Promise me something child," he said to her, "Promise me that you will not interfere with free will. It is very important that whatever you change will make things better. You must use your power only to further creation and not to cause it harm. Promise me," he repeated, "Promise me this, Hayada."

Part Two: A Test that Determined Fate

The bustling marketplace of Atheria thrummed with life, a vibrant tapestry of sights, sounds, and smells that assaulted Hayada's senses. She strolled through the crowd, her youthful form a stark contrast to the weathered faces of the merchants and farmers that surrounded her. Her eyes, bright with curiosity and a hint of mischief, darted from stall to stall, taking in the exotic wares, the vibrant fabrics, the tantalizing aromas of spices and roasted meats.

Hayada, still an adolescent in the grand scheme of godly lifespans, was eager to test the limits of her burgeoning powers. She had discovered her ability to manipulate reality, to alter perceptions, to weave illusions that could bend the very fabric of existence. But the full extent of her powers remained a tantalizing mystery, a challenge she was determined to unravel.

She paused beside a fruit vendor, his weathered hands carefully arranging a colorful display of apples, pears, and plums. Hayada focused her will, her mind reaching out to touch the vendor's thoughts, to glimpse into the depths of his consciousness.

But a frustrating barrier met her efforts, an impenetrable wall that blocked her access to his mind. She frowned, her brow furrowing in concentration. She tried again, her will intensifying, her power surging, but the barrier remained unyielding.

A surge of frustration washed over her, a childish petulance that belied her godly status. She wanted to know what the vendor was thinking, what secrets lay hidden within his mind. She wanted to reshape his reality, to weave an illusion that would transform his mundane existence into something extraordinary.

With a sudden impulse, she reached out, her hand gently touching the vendor's arm. A jolt of energy passed between them, and the barrier shattered, the vendor's thoughts laid bare before her like an open book.

Hayada gasped, her eyes widening with surprise and delight. She could see his worries about the dwindling harvest, his hopes for his daughter's upcoming marriage, his fleeting memories of a long-lost love.

She smiled, a mischievous glint in her eyes. With a playful twist of her will, she willed her powers into action, she made the vendor think of his lost love as a tyrannical influence he did not need in his life. She made him believe that if his daughter was alive and happy, that was all that mattered. She gave him confidence that his daughter would find a suitable husband, one that would love and cherish her for all time and that he need not worry about that eventuality.

The vendor's eyes widened in astonishment; his weathered face creased with a delighted smile. Hayada, basking in his wonder, reveled in the power she wielded, the ability to reshape reality with a mere touch, a fleeting thought.

As she withdrew her hand, she watched in amazement as the once grumpy and forlorn fruit vendor now sold his wares with excitement and joy, his customers enjoying his words and children flocking to his stall as he gave them apple slices, much to their delight. She searched for his thoughts again to see what they were like.

Hayada frowned, her brow furrowing in contemplation. She had discovered a crucial limitation to her powers. She could only manipulate the minds of those she touched, her influence confined to the realm of physical contact. She could not hear their thoughts, could not delve into their minds without bridging the gap between their physical forms.

It was a frustrating limitation, a tantalizing glimpse of a power she craved but could not fully grasp. But Hayada was not one to be deterred. She would find a way to overcome this obstacle, to unlock the full potential of her powers, to become the ultimate architect of reality.

Part Three: A Revelation and A Warning

The grand chamber of Dimarius hummed with a low thrum of divine energy, the air shimmering with iridescent light that danced across the smooth obsidian walls. Dimarius, his brow furrowed in contemplation, paced the length of the chamber, his heavy steps echoing in the vast silence.

Inflius, the wizened god of training, materialized beside him, his form radiating a calming aura of wisdom and experience. "You seem troubled, my friend," he observed, his voice a gentle rumble that echoed Dimarius's own unease.

Dimarius sighed, his shoulders slumping with the weight of his worries. "Hayada," he admitted, his voice heavy with concern. "Her powers... they are beyond anything I have witnessed before."

Inflius nodded, his eyes reflecting the flickering light of the chamber. "Indeed," he agreed. "She is... an anomaly."

He paused, his gaze turning towards the intricate tapestry that adorned the far wall, depicting the history of the gods and their eternal struggle against the forces of darkness. "Hayada's powers are twofold," he explained, his voice laced with a hint of awe. "She possesses the ability to manipulate minds, to alter perceptions, to weave illusions that can make mortals forget what was and perceive it to be something else entirely. She can alter their fates with a mere touch."

He turned back to Dimarius, his eyes filled with a grave concern. "But she also commands a more visceral power, a raw, untamed force that she can summon at will."

Dimarius's brow furrowed further. "I have witnessed this," he said, his voice laced with a hint of fear. "The creatures she conjures, the weapons she wields, the portals she opens... it is as if she commands the very essence of darkness."

Inflius nodded grimly. "Indeed," he confirmed. "Her powers are akin to those of... Horgon."

The name hung heavy in the air, a chilling reminder of the god who held the power of death, whose creations had threatened to plunge the world into an abyss of eternal darkness.

Dimarius's eyes widened in alarm. "Horgon?" he echoed, his voice barely a whisper. "But how is that possible?"

Inflius's gaze remained fixed on the tapestry, his eyes tracing the image of Horgon, his form wreathed in shadows, his hand gripping the fearsome Saber of Hiltar.

"Hayada's powers," he said, his voice grave, "are a mirror image of Horgon's. She is his legacy, his dark reflection in the grand tapestry of existence. If I didn't know any better Dimarius," Inflius said with an ominous pause, "I would wager that Hayada is a reincarnation of the Saber of Hiltar itself!"

A chilling silence descended upon the chamber, the weight of Inflius's words settling upon Dimarius like a shroud. Hayada, his daughter, the child he had hoped would bring balance to the world, was now a harbinger of chaos, a threat to the very fabric of existence.

CHAPTER

1

Opportunity Knocks

"The hardest day of any job is always the first day," said Jeremiah.

"You were always hesitant to try new things before you even know if you would like it or not, but now that you have been at it for four years, what do you think?" he asked.

"I still feel like this is not me," replied Josh. "But it keeps me busy, and it is not mundane so that part I actually enjoy."

"All I want is for you to be happy," said Jeremiah, "If being a journalist is not for you, then maybe you should keep looking? Don't settle for something less than ideal because that's how you make friends with regrets," he concluded.

"I won't," Josh said, "settle I mean," he added after a brief pause. "Now that we have had this riveting daily talk, I'm late for work so I will get going."

"Don't dismiss my parental concern young man," Jeremiah retorted, the smirk on his face belying his sarcasm, "They got you through high school and they will get you through your employment blues."

"Yes sir!" Josh replied, as he mockingly saluted his uncle. "Have a good day!"

The Mirage was one of the only remaining newspapers in the city that still upheld its core values of journalism. With an old school editor in chief, the journalists there were taught from day one to *seek the truth, speak the truth and be honest about it.* Josh never really understood what this motto meant but there was chivalry in the notion of honesty and that really called to him. The editor, Mr. Gerald Vargus, was eccentric at times but his intentions were always noble. To someone who did not know Mr. Vargus, he would have appeared to be a stubborn man in his fifties who insisted on getting his way. Not one to negotiate or barter with, Mr. Vargus was as straightforward a person as any. He would not sugarcoat his words, and he would not agree to portraying facts with added perspectives. "Facts are what happen," he would often say, "It is not your job to tell people how you feel about the facts, they are more than capable of forming opinions on their own." As a decorated veteran of journalism who had won many an award for his articles, Mr. Vargus commanded a certain respect within the journalism circles and among his staff. He ran his newspaper, the Mirage, with every intention of creating journalists in his own image.

The Mirage, for those reasons, wasn't the popular choice among the public. With people preferring sensationalized news over unadulterated facts, it was not every day that the Mirage received tips for stories, which meant they were not the first ones to report any exciting news, rather, they were just another paper that was clean. Although this outlook garnered everyone's respect and admiration, it also made it hard for the Mirage to pay their bills and pay their staff on time. Pay-cheques would be delayed for a week or two sometimes, but the staff didn't care as much so long as the pay kept coming.

Everyone there was only there because of Mr. Vargus. His leadership and insight meant there was a lot to learn from him and that was an opportunity that no young journalist wanted to miss. The Mirage was, therefore, a place that was often used as a steppingstone to success. A place where a journalist could put his or her foot in the proverbial door and learn the ropes, before seeking alternate, better paying employment.

The Mirage's office was in the older part of downtown in a building from the 1960's. Once known as the tallest building in the city, it was now dwarfed by its modern neighbors and yet, like the Mirage, it stood there, a landmark that nobody could ignore or forget. Having entered the lobby, Josh couldn't help but think of the outdated music that played in the elevator all day. He wondered what it would be like to spend a day to just go up and down, listening to the same song. One of the many cherished quirks his office had to offer, the elevator kept true to its old school charming self and was complete with creaky doors that often got stuck and buttons that did not work.

Anyone who worked at the Mirage knew to get off the elevator on the tenth floor and take the stairs to floor number eleven where their office was. A fact that nobody mentioned to Josh when he went for his interview. This trifling little detail also caused him to be late and Mr. Vargus was not happy about that. Josh thought how lucky he was to have gotten the job despite his tardiness. At the end of his interview, which was now four years ago, Mr. Vargus said, "You have a long way to go if you did not figure out a way around the elevator issue on time for your interview. But stick with me kid and I will make a fine journalist out of you yet."

As Josh absent mindedly climbed up the stairs and entered the Mirage's lobby, he noticed that the reception desk was empty. He could not recall the last time that had happened and thought it to be odd. He quickly dismissed it thinking the receptionist, Gary, probably quit from boredom and reached his desk only to find that the office was abuzz with excitement. Everyone was pouring into the conference room and Josh caught the attention of Adam, one of his more eager co-workers as he rushed past him.

"What's going on?" he asked, genuinely curious.

"We got a couple of tips on the hotline!" said Adam, not making any effort to conceal his excitement.

"That's rare," Josh replied.

"The early bird catches the worm my friend," Adam said as he rushed off to the conference room.

Josh quickly dropped off his satchel on his chair and hurried behind his excited friend. He went past the rows of desks, most of which were unoccupied, and into the conference room. He was one of the last ones to enter, which meant his chances of being handed one of the tips was slim to none. Curious, nonetheless, he found his spot at the table and sat down, waiting for Mr. Vargus to tell them what the fuss was all about.

"Is everyone here?" asked Mr. Vargus.

"Don't respond, that was rhetorical," he added, his gruff voice doing little to quell his own excitement. Josh had rarely seen this side of his grumpy boss and in a way, it made him think that Mr. Vargus would make a great Santa Claus at a Christmas party, if they ever had one. Reminding himself of how Mr. Vargus thought the holidays were when journalists had to be the most vigilant, lest they should let a good story escape them, he dismissed the thought of a jolly Mr. Vargus in a red suit as soon as it entered his mind.

"What are you smiling about Thompson?" asked the sharp Mr. Vargus.

As his train of thought came to an abrupt stop, Josh snapped himself out of his imagination and responded awkwardly, "Nothing, nothing," feeling everyone's eyes on him, he sheepishly added, "Nothing boss. I was just excited to hear what you have to say." Josh often wondered why Mr. Vargus referred to him by his last name. He had even made a list of reasons once just to pass the time and the most likely reason he could think of was that his first name was either not too journalistic or that his last name was too journalistic.

"Hmph," grunted Mr. Vargus, "Well if you are all done settling into your chairs, I would like to begin."

Clearing his throat, Mr. Vargus continued, "As you all know the tech giant, V5, announced last week that they were going to release a new product. While they haven't told anyone what this new product is going to be, you can bet that it will be something big."

V5 was a technology company that, in a very short amount of time, became involved with every major industry. Be it computers, cell phones, televisions, appliances, cars or software, V5 had a solution for everyone. Their rise to the top of the tech industry was unprecedented and solely because of their proprietary A.I software Kira. It was the most advanced A.I of its kind and experts were quoted to say that this is the closest A.I could ever get to mimicking human thought.

"As most of you know," Mr. Vargus explained, "We got a couple of tips, and they are both concerning V5's new product."

The conference room immediately erupted with excited whispers and gossip. This was indeed very big.

"Quiet down so I can tell you what I am talking about," Mr. Vargus interrupted, "We received a mysterious voicemail last night around 3 AM. The caller did not identify herself but sounded desperate. Rather than tell you what she said, I will now play the recording for you."

The room was silent with anticipation. Mr. Vargus walked over to the computer at the end and started the recording.

"V5 is going to ruin the world. There is something dreadfully wrong with their new earpiece and V5 will do everything in their power to stop the truth from getting out. I am calling you out of desperation and fear. I don't know if I will be alive long enough to explain everything to you. Please, you have to get this story out before it is too late! We only have a few weeks till it goes live! This thing has already killed people, and I can't live with that secret anymore!"

Then came the unmistakable 'click' sound that marked the end of the voicemail.

"I called the police myself as soon as I heard this voicemail and they assured me that it was a prank call," said Mr. Vargus diverting everyone's attention back to himself, "Needless to say, I feel like there is still merit in these leads. The two stories here are, one, about this earpiece thing and two, the proclaimed deaths. Although these two leads are related, I still want them both to run separately in the interest of time. V5 has a press conference scheduled for tomorrow morning and we need to get this news out by then. Ideally, we can report both of these stories online by tonight and in print for the morning."

That was a tall ask considering the amount of work that needed to go into a sensational story such as this. The legal backlash of tarnishing the name of the most powerful tech giant in the world was not to be trifled with. V5 could shut down the Mirage in a day if they chose to do so. Considering that risk, Mr. Vargus knew that the source had to be verified, and the stories written and proofread by 4 PM if they had a chance to get it out in time. If these leads proved to be true, the Mirage would be back in the limelight again. If they were dead ends, the Mirage would be done for good. That was a huge risk and Mr. Vargus was fully aware of the repercussions.

"As you have all done up until now," he said, "I ask that you trust my instincts about this story one more time. I don't have to tell you what might happen if we print this without proper verification. So, for that reason, I'm going to give the earpiece story to John Mason and the story about the deaths to Amy Smith."

That was no surprise. Josh knew one of those two was bound to get these leads. Both John and Amy had been with the Mirage for over fifteen years and they both had exceptional journalistic aptitude. If there were two individuals who lived the Mirage's motto of *seek the truth, speak the truth and be honest about it*, it was those two. Their stories reflected this philosophy to the core. The facts were always reported without bias and opinions were limited to personal reactions rather than courses of action.

"That is all I have for now," concluded Mr. Vargus, "John, Amy, I need you both to come to my office so we can discuss strategy. The rest of you can get back to work."

Josh knew that these were the kind of stories that made careers. He knew that if there was a chance for him to write even a part of these stories then he had to take it. His career, his reason for being a journalist, depended on writing breaking news pieces like this and he was not going to go back to his desk only to write another filler article about dog dander and pet allergies.

As the rest of his co-workers started to leave the conference room, Josh walked up to Mr. Vargus. "There is no way you are getting in on this without me," Adam said as he blocked Josh's path. "If you want a piece of this then I am tagging along!" he declared.

"Fine," replied Josh, "But we have to hurry!"

Adam and Josh made their way to Mr. Vargus who was busy packing up his notes. John and Amy both waited for him with their pens and notepads.

"Mr. Vargus, we need a minute," blurted out Adam.

The editor looked up, surprised to see two of his newer staff members not doing what he asked them to. "You two looking for something on my shirt?" he asked, "Because unless you want to write about my tailor, I suggest you get back to your desks."

"We would like to help with these leads," said Josh, "Mr. Vargus, we respect your decisions, and you know that, but we really want to help. If there is anything we can do, please let us. With all due respect to John and Amy, we can be useful if you can give us a chance."

The usually stoic expression on Mr. Vargus's face turned to one of intrigue and a smirk appeared where there was usually a grey moustache. Shaking his index finger at them he walked out from behind the computer, laughing heartily. "I get it," he said, "You want a shortcut to make your careers bloom like wildflowers," he continued as he put both his hands on Josh's shoulders, "But guess what happens to wildflowers in a city? They will be ripped out of the ground and be labelled as weeds. So, my answer is no."

"Mr. Vargus," Adam interjected, "Have I told you how wonderful you look in that blue shirt?" he said. Adam had an impeccable ability to anger Mr. Vargus and Josh never really understood why his jovial friend was still employed at the Mirage, considering the number of times he got screamed at. Mr. Vargus must've seen something unusually good to entertain a thorn in his side for as long as he did and continued to do so.

"Adam," Mr. Vargus replied, his expression turning to mild irritation, "I will not let your jokes ruin this day for me. I refuse to. So go back to your desks, the both of you, while they are still your desks!"

"Please Mr. Vargus," Josh insisted, "There has to be something more important that we can do besides writing filler articles. Please, I promise we will not disappoint you!"

Mr. Vargus was shocked at the persistence and possibly even taken aback. Josh and Adam waited for a few seconds that seemed like hours before they got a response, "You know," Mr. Vargus finally said as he started to walk toward the door, "I still can't give you either of these leads, but you can write a story about employee relations at V5 ahead of their big release."

"Thank you! Thank you!" Adam said, jumping up and down like a kid in a playground.

Mr. Vargus simply held up his hand as if to say 'enough of your antics' and continued, "If these leads turn out to be dead ends like the cops said, we will not print those stories and we will have a fallback article to say something about V5 that is insightful and informative. So, focus on that and while you both are there, you can learn from John and Amy."

"We won't disappoint you," Josh said. Although it was not what he expected, he knew that Mr. Vargus wouldn't just hand him a story that was intended for the most seasoned journalists on staff. He felt happy that his persistence paid dividends. At the very least, it meant he wouldn't have to waste his time on an article that would only serve to fill space on the paper. Being able to see how John and Amy go about their work was an invaluable learning opportunity. Perhaps this would be the push Josh needed to finally fall in love with journalism he thought.

Mr. Vargus simply nodded and continued, "Now get to work and don't bother me again until your story is ready to read," he said as he walked toward his office with John and Amy.

"This is so awesome!" Adam said to Josh.

"We didn't get the leads," Josh replied, his tone of voice conveying the obviousness of the situation.

"No, we did not," Adam continued, the smile on his face growing bigger by the second, "But I have a contact at V5."

Josh's eyes widened, "Do you really?" he asked, attempting to hide his excitement.

"My friend works there, and I can get us access into the building," Adam said, "And with any luck, the two of us can get 'the scoop' on both of these leads before John or Amy can and with any luck, may be even get a quote or two from their CEO, Hayada Dartilla, and then!" he said as his hands motioned an airplane taking off, "We just sit back and watch our careers skyrocket!" He held out his hand to Josh, standing squarely in front of him, "So what do you say partner? Ready for this rollercoaster?"

"You bet!" replied Josh as he shook Adam's hand. They both grabbed their notepads, pens and recorders and headed out the door.

CHAPTER

2

The Lead that Developed

The V5 campus was abuzz with excitement that morning. Everyone there, every employee, every vendor and every visitor could feel the palpable anticipation. Adam's cousin, Fernando was not happy or even remotely 'OK' with the favor that Adam had asked of him. In fact, he wanted nothing to do with it at all. He was a clerk at the public relations office and the best he could do was get Adam and Josh in touch with someone they could talk to but even that was a gross violation of policy that could result in him losing his job.

The risk of this deed being heavy in itself, what Adam did to keep Fernando out of jail for a possession charge that occurred a few years ago, there was no way he could say no. He had to help Adam so he would not owe him anything anymore.

Having arrived at the V5 office, Adam and Josh waited for Fernando to greet them. When fifteen minutes turned into an hour, they started to grow impatient.

"How long do you think we should wait for your cousin?" Josh interrupted, "He did not seem very happy to help us at all."

"I think we should just go inside and see who we can find," said Adam, "Like every great reporter based in fiction, I think we have to find our own story."

"Ready for this?" Adam asked, a mischievous grin spreading across his face.

"Absolutely," Josh replied, trying to mask his nervousness with a confident smile.

They approached the entrance, a revolving door that whooshed as it spun. Inside, the lobby was a hive of activity, with employees rushing back and forth, their faces illuminated by the glow of their smartphones.

"This way," Adam said, leading Josh toward a bank of elevators. They stepped inside, and Adam pressed the button for the 14th floor.

As the elevator ascended, Josh's heart pounded in his chest. He couldn't believe he was actually here, at the heart of V5, the company that was changing the world with its cutting-edge technology. The doors opened, and they stepped out onto a plushily carpeted hallway. Adam led Josh down the hall, past a series of conference rooms and offices, until they reached a door marked "Public Relations." Adam knocked, and a moment later, the door opened. A woman with a warm smile and a neatly pressed suit stood in the doorway.

"Hello," she said, "I'm Sarah. You must be the reporters from The Mirage."

"That's right," Adam replied, "I'm Adam, and this is Josh." He quickly glanced over at his nervous friend and whispered, "Just go along with the flow. I think she thinks we are John and Amy, and I think we should let her think that! Clearly Mr. Vargus didn't tell her our names."

"Welcome to V5," Sarah said, "Please come in."

They stepped inside, and Sarah led them to a small conference room. The room was sparsely furnished, with a table and a few chairs.

"Can I offer you anything to drink?" Sarah asked.

"No, thank you," Josh replied, "We're fine."

"Alright then," Sarah said, "Let's get started."

She sat down at the table, and Josh and Adam took their seats across from her.

"So," Sarah began, "I understand you're here to do a story on V5's new product."

"That's right," Adam replied, "We're very interested in learning more about it."

"Well," Sarah said, "I'm afraid I can't tell you much at this point. The product is still under wraps, and we're not ready to release any details yet."

"That's understandable," Josh said, "But we were hoping you could give us a sneak peek."

"I'm afraid not," Sarah replied, "But I can tell you that it's going to be a game-changer. It's going to revolutionize the way we interact with technology."

"That's quite a claim," Adam said, "Can you give us any hints?"

"I'm afraid not," Sarah replied, "But I can tell you that it's going to be worth the wait."

Josh and Adam exchanged glances. They were getting nowhere with Sarah. They needed to find another way to get information about V5's new product.

"Well," Adam said, "We appreciate your time, Sarah. But we're hoping you can help us with something else."

"What's that?" Sarah asked.

"We're also interested in learning more about V5's employee relations," Adam replied, "We've heard some rumors that there have been some problems."

"Rumors?" Sarah asked, her eyebrows raised.

"Yes," Josh said, "We've heard that there have been some issues with employee morale."

"I'm afraid I can't comment on that," Sarah replied, "But I can tell you that V5 is a great place to work. We offer our employees a competitive salary and benefits package, and we're committed to creating a positive and supportive work environment."

"That's good to hear," Adam said, "But we're still interested in learning more about the rumors."

"I'm afraid I can't help you with that. This is the first I am hearing about this, which only tells me that they are what you say they are, rumours," Sarah replied, "But I can assure you that V5 is a company that cares about its employees." Sarah then stood up and walked over to the door, "Well if there is nothing else gentlemen, I hope you have a great day!" she said as she opened the door for them to leave.

"Well," Adam said, "We appreciate your time, Sarah. But we're hoping you can put us in touch with someone who can answer our questions."

"I'm afraid not," Sarah replied, "But I can offer you a tour of V5's headquarters. That might give you a better sense of our company culture."

"That would be great," Josh said, "We'd love to see V5's headquarters."

"Alright then," Sarah said, "Please follow me."

She led them out of the conference room and into the hallway. They followed her down the hall, past a series of offices and cubicles, until they reached a large open space.

"This is our employee lounge," Sarah explained, "It's where our employees come to relax and socialize."

The lounge was a hive of activity, with employees playing games, chatting, and eating lunch. Amidst a sea of happy go lucky techies, Josh noticed a nervous face. There was someone in that room that did not like being there and had a fearful expression on her face which was a stark contrast to every other lively and joyful smile in the room.

"Who is that?" Josh asked, his curiosity not making any efforts to hide.

"Oh that is the busiest person in this building today," replied Sarah, "That's Miranda Hawthorne, the project manager for the Vbuddy earpiece."

"Can we talk to her for a few minutes quickly?" Adam interjected," Please, it would mean so much to our story."

"I am sorry but no," replied Sarah, "We are all under strict orders not to talk about this project until its release. You can attend the press conference with the rest of the journalists to find out more. Once you get to the lobby, please do register for it at the front desk and collect your press passes."

"So you are calling it the Vbuddy," Josh said.

"We are," Sarah replied, an angry smirk starting to spread on her face. She had no intention of letting that information slip, "But I have to insist that we move on now as I do have a meeting to attend in a couple of hours."

They continued their tour, and Sarah showed them V5's cutting-edge manufacturing facilities, and its expansive employee cafeteria.

"V5 is an impressive company," Josh said.

"It is," Sarah replied, "We're changing the world."

As their tour concluded, Josh and Adam thanked Sarah for her time. They still didn't have any concrete information about V5's new product but they now knew what it was called and who the project manager was. They left V5 headquarters and stepped back out onto the sidewalk. The sun was shining, and the city was bustling with activity.

"Well," Adam said, "That was a bust."

"Not entirely," Josh replied, "We learned a lot about V5."

"True," Adam said, "But we still don't have a story."

"We will," Josh said, "We just need to find a way to talk to Miranda Hawthorne."

They walked down the street, their minds racing. They needed to find a way to get the scoop on V5's new product.

As they walked, they passed a small coffee shop. They decided to stop in and get a cup of coffee.

They sat down at a table, and Adam pulled out his notebook.

"Alright," he said, "Let's brainstorm."

They spent the next hour discussing possible ways to get information about V5. They considered contacting former employees, interviewing industry experts, and even trying to hack into V5's computer system.

"I think I have an idea," Josh said finally.

"What's that?" Adam asked.

"We need to wait for Miranda to leave the building and then follow her," Josh replied, "Once we are clear of the V5 campus, we can approach her and see if she wants to talk."

"That's a good idea," Adam said, "But how are we going to stalk a project manager at V5 without getting noticed?"

"Don't ask me!" Josh replied, "This whole thing was your idea, wasn't it? I am sure you can come up with a way for us to follow someone without being noticed."

Adam's expression changed from mildly curious to animated decisiveness. "The press passes!" he said as he pumped his fist in the air.

"What about them?" Josh asked, not at all certain of this revelation his friend just had.

"If V5 gives us press passes and we show them to Miranda, she might be more inclined to talk to us because the passes were given to us," Adam said as Josh clued in and finished the sentence, "by V5!"

They both stood up and did a celebratory high five making no effort to hide their enthusiasm, much to the chagrin of the other patrons at the café. Gathering their belongings, Adam and Josh made their way to the till to pay for their coffees.

"Are you both reporters?" asked the surly man who was settling their bill.

"Yes, we are," replied Adam, "We are with the mirage."

"Your coffees are on the house then," replied the man as he handed a receipt to Adam, "Have a nice day!"

Relishing their good fortune and feeling a sense of pride at the work they did, Adam and Josh started to walk back to the V5 headquarters, they passed a group of people protesting outside of V5 headquarters. The protesters were holding signs that read "V5 is exploiting its employees" and "V5 is destroying our privacy." Josh observed the protesters and could not help but wonder if the real story here was about the earpiece or the employee relations issue. Or perhaps, were the two leads interconnected somehow. They made their way through the ornate revolving door once more and approached the front desk.

"Hi there," Adam said to the young lady busy typing away on her computer, "We are reporters here to cover the release of the new earpiece and would like to register ourselves for the press conference."

"I can definitely help you with that," she said, "My name is Emily. Which news outlet are you from?" she asked.

"We're from The Mirage," Adam said.

"Alrighty," Emily replied, as he typed away on her computer. Shortly after she printed out press passes and handed them to Adam and Josh. "The press conference is taking place at the conference hall on the 14th floor tonight at 6 PM. There is a cocktail party starting at 4 if you would like to attend as well."

"Is Miranda Hawthorne also going to be in attendance?" Josh asked.

"Of course," Emily replied, "All project managers who worked on the hardware and the software will be present and able to answer questions at the event."

"Thank you for your time," replied Josh and led Adam out of the building.

"So we are going to the party, right?" asked Adam, his mischievous grin plastered on his face.

"No we are not!" retorted Josh, "We are going to find Miranda before she gets to the party and talk to her."

"Not before I post a photo of this amazing receipt for the world to see how much we are appreciated!" giggled Adam. As he opened the receipt to take a picture, he froze. His expression changed from glee to serious thought.

"We cannot talk about V5 here, meet me at 1653 Blairwood Cove at 2 PM," said the note on the receipt.

The man who handed them the receipt, quietly withdrew to the back office of the café. He sat down at his desk and let out a confused sigh. "I did it," he said.

"Thank you," replied Miranda. She stood up from the spare chair in the office and left the café from the back entrance.

CHAPTER

3

The Floor without Cameras

The elevator doors slid open with a soft whoosh, and Miranda stepped out onto the 37th floor. V5 headquarters was a monument to modern architecture, all gleaming steel and glass, but this morning, the sleek surroundings felt more like a gilded cage. Her heart hammered against her ribs, a frantic drumbeat against the silence of the deserted hallway. It was barely 7:00 AM, and the floor was eerily quiet, the usual bustle of early-arriving employees replaced by an unsettling stillness.

Miranda hugged her laptop bag closer, her knuckles white against the worn leather. Every soft click of her heels on the polished floor seemed to echo in the vast emptiness, amplifying her sense of isolation. She hadn't slept a wink last night, the weight of her suspicion pressing down on her like a physical burden. Her assistant, Edward had not been to work since the day she asked him to visit the head researcher, Dominic Flyhauser to find out why there were discrepancies in the code they submitted for the Vbuddy project versus the code that was in the actual project draft.

If that was not suspicious enough, the project manager that Miranda herself replaced, Mithila Sivanayagam, had also left the company abruptly after a clandestine meeting to clarify similar doubts. V5 took pride in every project manager having their own video log of how their days were going. The emphasis here being the mental wellbeing of every employee of V5, these video logs were reviewed, *'confidentially,'*

19

by the human resources department, specifically the employee wellness coordinators who then contacted specific individuals to talk further about what was recorded in these logs.

Miranda always felt this to be an invasion of privacy but V5 being the global technology superpower that it was, she never thought to question their motives or agendas.

There were reports of other employees who randomly either left the company or went on extended sabbaticals and never returned, mysteriously, all connected to the Vbuddy project. This was circumstantial at best and so Miranda had resolved to find out the truth for herself. Fueled by a growing unease and concern for her own life and well-being, she'd finally given in to her suspicions. She had to know what was happening on the 50th floor. Miranda organized a late-night meeting for the offsite marketing department to meet with their own marketing coordinators to discuss the launch of Vbuddy overseas and to build a budget model for the same. It was the perfect cover since she did not have to directly get involved in the discussions. She could silently, '*join the conference call*' and pretend to be present as she conducted her covert sting operation.

While her colleagues were occupied with budget reports and marketing strategies, she'd slipped away, her heart pounding with a mixture of fear and determination. The research lab on the 50th floor was a restricted area that required special clearance. But Miranda, as project manager, had access.

She'd used her ID card to bypass the security checkpoint, her hand trembling as she swiped it through the reader. The heavy steel door hissed open, and she stepped into a world that chilled her to the bone. She walked through the doors expecting the floor to be busy and abuzz with people and machine noises but to her shock, it was quiet. Not a single room had anyone in it and yet the entry log where she swiped her key card said there were 93 occupants on the floor. She walked through the deserted floor of labs, taking pictures in every room and noting down whatever looked out of place. Her suspicions only grew stronger when she noticed that there were no security cameras anywhere on the floor. None of the corridors, hallways or labs had any security cameras. It was as if V5 did not want their own employees or managers to know what was actually happening there.

As she walked to the end of the hallway, she could feel the temperature dropping sharply. She thought it was odd but kept going, reassuring herself that the cooler temperature was probably to keep the computers from overheating. Then she saw it. The room at the end. The cold brass doors and dim lights only added to the eeriness and fear that were building inside her. Her breath visibly faster as vapor escaped her clattering mouth with every step. The chill she felt was deeper, darker and more frightening than the mere temperature difference. She was not looking at a broom closet or storage space. The chair with chains attached to the arm rests, the table strewn with blunt objects and the jar of teeth and fingernails atop the shelves could only mean one thing. The room was reeking of fear and suffering only because it was a torture chamber.

Domic Flyhauser, the head researcher for the Vbuddy project had once mentioned that he wanted to advance A.I to such an extent that whoever interacted with Kira the V5 A.I would not be able to tell the difference between Kira and a real person. That meant that Kira would need to understand and be able to replicate human emotions such as loyalty, affection, empathy, sympathy and also, fear. But nothing could have prepared Miranda for the reality of it. The bloodstains on the floor, the restraints on the chair, the lingering scent of something metallic and acrid... it was a scene straight out of a nightmare.

She crept closer to the chair, each step a victory over her rising panic. The room was small, the air thick with a metallic tang that made her stomach churn. A single bare bulb hung from the ceiling, casting harsh shadows that danced and writhed with her every move. The chair, bolted to the floor, was cold, unforgiving steel. Leather straps dangled from the arms and legs, worn smooth with use.

Miranda raised her phone, the camera lens a single, unblinking eye. She documented everything: the rusty shackles hanging from the ceiling, the array of instruments laid out on a stainless-steel tray – pliers, scalpels, things she couldn't even name. Each photo was a piece of evidence, a testament to the horrors hidden within these walls.

As she backed away, her heel bumped against something solid. She whirled around, her heart leaping into her throat. The door. It was closing, the heavy steel sliding shut with a terrifying finality. Panic clawed at her, her breath catching in ragged gasps. She fumbled for the handle, but it was no use. The door was locked.

She was trapped.

A wave of dizziness washed over her, and she sank to the floor, her back pressed against the cold steel. She had to get out of here. She had to tell someone. But how? She frantically pulled out her cellphone to call for help but there was no signal. She could not dial out. She could not even connect to the local emergency number. The thoroughness of V5 at keeping this torture chamber a secret sank in to her being. The fear of losing her life grew with every passing moment.

Then, through the thick metal, she heard it. A muffled scuffling, a desperate cry, the sickening thud of flesh against metal. Someone was being dragged down the hallway.

The sounds grew louder, closer. Miranda scrambled to her feet, her eyes darting around the room, searching for an escape, a hiding place. There was nowhere to go.

The footsteps stopped right outside the door. Miranda pressed herself against the wall, her body trembling, her breath held hostage in her lungs. She could hear the grunts and groans, the sharp intake of breath between pained cries. Then, a voice, low and menacing, spitting out words she couldn't understand.

The door creaked open. Miranda darted away from the door and hid behind a metal shelf close by. The one advantage she had in this otherwise hopeless scenario was that the door of the torture chamber, being as heavy and menacing as it is, would take time to open. She was able to go fully out of sight before being noticed. However, aside from the fleeting moment of solace of not being instantly discovered, there was nothing she could do to quell the eventuality that her mind kept reminding her of. The inevitability of her impending doom of when, not if, she would be discovered by whoever was entering that dreaded room.

Miranda squeezed her eyes shut, her fingers digging into the cold steel wall. She couldn't look. She couldn't bear to witness whatever horrors were about to unfold.

But curiosity, that primal urge to know, overcame her fear. Slowly, she opened her eyes, peering through a crack in the shelf.

Two men, their faces obscured by shadows, were dragging a limp figure into the room. Miranda's blood ran cold. She recognized the expensive shoes, the tailored suit.

Edward.

They strapped him to the chair, his body slack, his head lolling to one side. He was unconscious. Or dead.

Miranda's stomach lurched. She had to do something. She had to help him.

But what could she do?

She was just one woman, trapped in a soundproof room, facing two ruthless men who clearly had no qualms about inflicting pain.

The men exchanged a few words, their voices too low for Miranda to decipher. Then, one of them picked up a scalpel from the tray. He approached Edward, the blade glinting ominously in the dim light.

Miranda's scream died in her throat. She couldn't watch this. She couldn't bear to see Edward suffer.

She turned away, pressing her hands over her ears, trying to block out the sounds of Edward's agony. But the images, the sounds, the smells, they were all burned into her memory, a horrifying spectacle she would never be able to erase.

She had to get out of there. She had to escape.

She fumbled with her phone, her fingers shaking so badly she could barely hold it steady. Remembering to turn off her flash and sounds, she clicked as many pictures of Edward's horrors as she could. She whispered a desperate plea for help, her voice choked with tears.

Then, she did the only thing she could think of. Gingerly, she picked up an empty jar from the shelf, shivering, quaking in fear and threw it out of the open door. The men paused; their attention momentarily diverted. One of them went outside to see what the commotion was, followed by the second man.

Miranda stared at them, her heart beating faster than a race car, begging, pleading with lady luck to give her an opportunity to survive. The men picked up the broken shards of glass and looked around to see where the jar had come from. Noticing the cart of jars next to the door they looked back down, content with the understanding that it probably fell off the cart and started to clean up. Miranda grabbed another jar from the shelf, this one full of human teeth, and made her way to the door that led out of the torture chamber.

Watching Edward unconscious, a mere twenty feet from where she hid, did nothing to quell her fear. She fumbled around and produced the jar of teeth she took and threw it at Edward's chair. The two men, confused and alerted, darted back into the room to examine Edward. One of them, clearly angry, pushed the other man and said something about putting keepsakes away properly to ensure they don't have to clean up more than needed. Bewildered still, they knelt and started to pick up the teeth and shattered glass from the ground. Before they had a chance to look around the room, Miranda stumbled out into the hallway, her legs shaky, her vision blurred. She didn't look back. She just ran. Thanking her stars that the two men were not smart enough to think of an intruder being present, she ran.

She ran until she couldn't run anymore, until her lungs burned, and her legs ached. She collapsed in a stairwell, her body wracked with sobs.

The guilt was crushing. She had left Edward behind. She had abandoned him to his fate. She now knew the fate of anyone who dared to know more. Mustering whatever strength she had left in her soul, she went back to her office and sat down. It was barely midnight, but she knew she had to do something. Her ID card was used to access the research department. V5 already knew she was there. She had to let someone know.

Her desk phone rang, interrupting her dazed brainstorming. Composing herself as best she could, Miranda answered, "Miranda Hawthorne speaking," she said in as calm a voice as she could muster.

"Good evening Ms. Hawthorne, this is the building security office. We noticed you went to the R&D floor; I trust your visit was good?" said the voice. Miranda was right. They knew. They knew she had been there. What they didn't know was what she saw. If they did, she would not be receiving a phone call, she would have received a bullet in her head or worse, the torture chamber.

"Regretfully, no," she replied, doing her best to feign frustration, "I went to meet Dr. Flyhauser but there was nobody there. I waited for a while and came back. I will just have to meet with him tomorrow."

"We are sorry to hear that. Please do call us next time and we can arrange a visit with Dr. Flyhauser. He is a very busy man and unannounced visits like this are discouraged by him," said the security office.

"I will keep that in mind. Thank you for your call," Miranda replied and ended the phone call.

Breathing a sigh of relief, she drank some water. Feeling her heart calming down, she sat down to devise a plan on how to expose V5 but more importantly, how she can bring them to justice for all the horrible things they have done and continue to do. Edward was surely not the first person in that chair and is likely not the last either. She spent the next two hours thinking about what she had to do. She did not write anything down and she did not say anything out loud.

She removed the SIM card from her phone. She then turned off the wifi in her laptop and connected her phone to it. She made copies of the photos she had taken and saved them on her laptop. Clutching her laptop and her phone she then left the building. She got into her car and drove for what felt like an hour through the empty streets. There were hardly any people out and about at 3 A.M., in the morning. When she felt she was far enough away from V5, she stopped at a payphone. She then called the only newspaper she could think of. The only newspaper that still sounded genuine or had integrity. She called the Mirage. She did not expect anyone to answer the phone, but she had to say something. She had to get someone to start looking into V5. There was no telling if she would be alive long enough to follow all the rules and alert the proper authorities. She had no idea how far V5's influence extended that they would be brazen enough to have a torture chamber in the very building where all their employees worked. When the automated message said to leave a voicemail after the beep, she did:

> *"V5 is going to ruin the world. There is something dreadfully wrong with their new earpiece and V5 will do everything in their power to stop the truth from getting out. I am calling you out of desperation and fear. I don't know if I will be alive long enough to explain everything to you. Please, you must get this story out before it is too late! This thing has already killed people, and I can't live with that secret anymore!"*

She went back home and copied the photos from her laptop onto a disposable thumb drive and deleted them from her computer. Being a software engineer in her own regard, she knew how to wipe her digital footprints. She knew how to make her laptop seem as if no pictures had ever been saved to it or copied away from it. After covering her tracks and deleting the photos from her phone, she put the SIM card back into her phone. She then proceeded to get ready to go back to V5.

She had to. She had to go back to prevent suspicion and to wait for reporters from the Mirage to come by so she could talk to them. That afternoon, when she saw them walking around the employee lounge with Sarah, she knew they got her voicemail. Now she had to make sure they found the evidence. She left the building along with Adam and Josh, making sure to keep her distance as she followed them to the café. She went inside the café from the back entrance and found the owner, Greg. A big surly man with a passion for helping his friends.

"Sorry Ms. Hawthorne," he said with a confused look in his eyes, "You seem to be lost. I will need you to go back to the guest area. This is for employees only."

"I need your help, Greg!" she said to him. Her tone serious enough to convey to him that she was in deep trouble.

"This is very unusual Ms. Hawthorne," he replied, "I have never seen you like this. Is everything alright?"

"There is no time to explain Greg. See those two reporters who just sat down?" she asked him.

"Yes," he questioned, as he gave Adam and Josh a quick glance from behind the curtain.

"I need you to charge me for whatever they are drinking or eating. But still give them a receipt. On the back of the receipt, I need you to write this down." She gave him a note.

"Don't ask me anything Greg," she added before he could complain, "This is very important."

"Alright Ms. Hawthorne," Greg replied, sounding resigned, "I will do as you ask."

CHAPTER

4

The Empty Apartment

Josh and Adam arrived at 1653 Blairwood Cove, a nondescript apartment building in a quiet residential neighborhood. The address, scribbled hastily on the receipt, felt out of place in the peaceful setting. A sense of unease settled over them as they climbed the stairs, their footsteps echoing in the empty hallway.

They found the apartment door slightly ajar. Adam pushed it open, and they cautiously stepped inside. The apartment was small and sparsely furnished, with a worn couch, a flickering television, and a cluttered coffee table. It looked like it hadn't been lived in for a while.

"Hello?" Adam called out, his voice echoing in the silence. There was no answer.

They exchanged nervous glances. They were expecting to meet someone there. Perhaps the man from the café who gave them the receipt. Or even better, Miranda herself. But to find that there was nobody there was a little unsettling. Who wanted to meet them? Who passed the message through the receipt? As they scanned the room, Josh noticed a small envelope on the floor near the coffee table. He picked it up. Inside was a small thumb drive and a key card.

"What do you think this is?" he asked, holding it up.

Adam shrugged, "No idea. Maybe it's Miranda's?"

They decided to take the drive back to The Mirage office and see what it contained. Back at their desks, they connected the drive to a laptop. A single video file appeared on the screen.

They clicked on it, and Miranda's face filled the screen. Her eyes were filled with fear and determination as she spoke directly to the camera. She explained her growing suspicions about V5, the disappearances of her colleagues, and her late-night exploration of the research labs. She described the torture chamber in chilling detail, her voice trembling with emotion.

Then, the video cut to a series of photos. The images were grainy and poorly lit, but clear enough to show the horrors Miranda witnessed: the bloodstains on the floor, the restraints on the chair, the instruments of torture laid out on the tray.

Josh and Adam stared at the screen, their faces pale with shock. They couldn't believe what they were seeing. V5, the company that promised to revolutionize the world, was hiding a dark and sinister secret.

The video ended with Miranda pleading for them to expose the truth, to stop V5 before it was too late.

"I don't know how much longer I can keep myself safe," she said in the video, "But I trust you to do the right thing."

Josh and Adam exchanged a determined look. They knew what they had to do. They had to expose V5, no matter the cost. That discovery raised the stakes and added a new layer of urgency to their mission. They now had concrete evidence of V5's crimes, but they also knew that Miranda was in grave danger. They had to act fast.

Adam's hand hovered over the phone; his finger poised to dial. "We have to tell Mr. Vargus," he said, his voice urgent. "This is huge!"

Josh grabbed his wrist, his grip firm. "Wait," he said, his brow furrowed in thought. "We need to be smart about this."

Adam looked at him, puzzled. "What do you mean?"

"If this video is real," Josh explained, "Miranda's life is in danger. We can't risk exposing her without knowing she's safe."

Adam's eyes widened. "You think V5 might have already..." he trailed off, unable to finish the sentence.

Josh nodded grimly. "It's possible. Or they could try to discredit her, make her seem unstable, or even worse, frame her for something."

"But we have the video," Adam protested. "The photos, the evidence..."

Josh shook his head. "It's not enough. V5 could easily claim it's fabricated, a hoax to damage their reputation. There is no way someone could connect these photos to V5. We only think this because of what Miranda said in the video. If you remove the video from the equation, which, by the way, can become a 'he said she said' conspiracy video, there is nothing in these photos to prove that this torture chamber is actually in V5 or is being run by V5. Without Miranda to corroborate the story, or without concrete proof that connects this torture chamber to that company, we don't have a case."

Adam slumped back in his chair, deflated. "So, what do we do?"

Josh's eyes gleamed with determination. "We go to the cocktail party. We find Miranda. We make sure she's safe, and we get her to confirm everything on the record."

Adam sat up, a spark of excitement reigniting in his eyes. "And then we blow this whole thing wide open."

Josh nodded. "Exactly. But first, we need a plan."

Adam and Josh got up and ready to leave as Mr. Vargus approached their desk, "And where do you think you two are going?" He asked.

"Just doing our jobs chief," replied Josh doing his best to disguise the look on his face, "We got an invite to the cocktail party at V5 so we wanted to go and see what we can find," he trailed off as Mr. Vargus raised his hand.

"You two got there before your leads. Because of the stunt you pulled, John and Amy cannot be there for the press conference. Now while I have half a mind to fire you both, I will give you one chance to tell me why you both deserve to keep your jobs!" he said, his arms crossed, his expression resolute.

"Chief, we found some evidence to say that V5 is up to some shady stuff," Adam said, ignoring the stern looks Josh was throwing his way. "I know what you're going to say so let me say it first. We cannot print this story without solid evidence which is what we are about to get right now. If we get this evidence, it will expose a massive conspiracy and bring justice to a lot of people, but we need to leave now to do that."

Mr. Vargus kept staring at them both. His expression, unmoving and his arms still folded. "You can follow your story." He finally said, "But you are still suspended for a week once you come back and that is if this turns into a printable story to begin with. If you strike out today, you can forget your careers."

"Thanks chief!" replied Josh without hesitation, "We won't let you down!" Adam and Josh quickly grabbed their bags and the thumb drive and left the Mirage. Mr. Vargus's warning still resonated in their minds, but their jobs seemed like a small price to pay for saving Miranda's life and that was a decision that both of them were more than happy to live with.

Ensuring to follow the dress code listed for the cocktail party, they both wore black tuxedos and made their way back to V5. They showed the security guards their press passes and went up to the 14th floor and entered the gigantic conference room that was turned into a cocktail bar with tables and assigned seating for all the attendees.

The party swirled around them, a cacophony of clinking glasses, forced laughter, and vapid conversation. Josh and Adam navigated the crowded room, their eyes scanning the smiling faces, searching for Miranda. But she was nowhere to be found.

Anxiety gnawed at them. Looking around for a familiar face they finally saw Sarah. The not so helpful public relations officer they met that morning.

"Hey Sarah!" exclaimed Adam, "This is quite the party you guys are throwing!" he said, doing his best to appear as impressed as possible at the lavish and over-the-top cocktail party. "By the way," he added, "I was hoping to meet Miranda Hawthorne, you wouldn't happen to be kind enough to point her out to us, would you?" he asked her, as charmingly as he possibly could.

"Miranda is unwell," Sarah replied. A very curt and matter of fact tone of finality in her voice. "Regretfully, she will not be attending the party or the press conference after. But if you would like to speak to her, I am sure that can be arranged after the product launch happens in a few weeks."

It was a thinly veiled excuse, an affirmation of their worst fears. Miranda was missing. She was likely in that torture chamber, suffering a fate too horrible to imagine. They had to act fast. There was no time to alert the police, no time to gather reinforcements. Miranda's life hung in the balance.

Adam's eyes darted around the room, searching for an escape route, a way to reach Miranda. Then, he remembered the key card they had found in the envelope with the thumb drive. Could it be their ticket to the 50th floor?

"Josh," he whispered, his voice urgent, "the key card! Maybe it gives us access to the research labs."

Josh's eyes widened. "It's worth a shot," he said. "Let's get out of here."

They slipped away from the party unnoticed, their hearts pounding with a mixture of fear and determination. They found a service elevator and used the key card to authorize the security panel. The elevator lurched upwards, carrying them towards the unknown.

As the elevator reached the 50th floor, a sense of dread washed over them. The hallway was eerily silent, the only sound the hum of the ventilation system. They crept down the corridor, their footsteps muffled by the plush carpet.

They reached the door to the research department. It was the moment of truth. Josh pulled out the key card they found in the envelope and swiped it against the card reader. The next moment felt longer than an entire day, perhaps an entire week but a slight swell of relief crept into their minds as the card reader blinked green followed by the unmistakable click of the door unlocking itself.

"Ready?" he whispered.

Adam nodded; his jaw clenched. "Let's do this."

They pushed the door open and stepped into the darkness, ready to face whatever horrors awaited them.

CHAPTER

5

The Lingering Light

Josh and Adam, their hearts pounding like drums in their chests, crept through the dimly lit corridors of the research department. Every lab they passed, empty yet full of machinery. Not a soul in sight and yet the entire floor felt alive with fear and nervousness, palpable and evident as the chill of helplessness swept through them with cold unwavering inevitability. The air was thick with tension, and every little noise they heard seemed to amplify their anxieties. With a mix of fear, anger and determination fueling their every step, they walked through the hallway as the temperature kept getting colder with every step.

Finally, they reached a heavy metal door, its surface marred with deep scratches and gouges. This had to be it.

"I wonder what made these scratches," Josh remarked.

"What scratches?" Adam replied, clearly confused by what his friend said. "Don't let the cold play tricks on you," he concluded.

With a deep breath, Josh braced himself and shoved against the door. It creaked open with a silent groan, revealing a dark, cavernous room. The hallway being dimly lit, opening the door did little to distract its inhabitants. Adam and Josh carefully peered inside. The sight that greeted them was both horrifying and heartbreaking. Miranda was strapped to a chair in the center of the room, her face pale and drawn, her eyes filled with fear and pain. Dominic Flyhauser, his face contorted in a cruel sneer, stood before her, a wicked glint in his eyes.

"Who did you speak to?" Dominic snarled, his voice dripping with venom. "What did you tell them?"

Miranda remained silent; her lips pressed into a thin line. She knew that anything she said would only put Josh and Adam in danger.

Dominic's face contorted in rage. He grabbed a nearby metal rod and raised it menacingly over Miranda's head.

"I will make you talk," he hissed.

Just as Dominic was about to bring the rod down on Miranda, Josh and Adam burst into the room. They had been watching from the shadows, their blood boiling at the sight of Miranda's suffering.

With a synchronized yell, they lunged at Dominic, tackling him to the ground. The metal rod clattered to the floor, its clang echoing through the room.

A fierce struggle ensued. Josh and Adam, fueled by adrenaline and rage, rained blows upon Dominic, their fists connecting with his face and body. Dominic fought back with surprising strength, but he was no match for their combined fury.

Finally, Josh managed to land a solid punch to Dominic's jaw, sending him sprawling to the ground. He lay there unconscious, his face a bloody mess.

Josh and Adam rushed to Miranda's side, untying the straps that bound her to the chair. She was weak and trembling, but she was alive.

"Are you alright?" Josh asked, his voice thick with concern.

Miranda nodded weakly. "I'm... I'm...," she stammered.

"We need to get out of here," Adam said urgently. "Before someone finds us."

With Miranda leaning on Josh for support, they made their way out of the torture chamber. They moved quickly and quietly, their hearts pounding in their chests. They knew that they couldn't stay in V5 headquarters any longer. They had to get Miranda to safety.

As they made their way through the corridors, they heard the sound of approaching footsteps. They quickened their pace, their breaths coming in ragged gasps. They had to find a way out of the building before they were caught.

They reached a dead end, a locked door blocking their escape. They were trapped.

Just as they were about to give up hope, they heard a voice coming from the other side of the door.

"Josh? Adam? Is that you?"

It was Sarah. She had been searching for them since they went missing from the cocktail party.

"Sarah!" Josh cried out in relief. "We're trapped!"

Sarah fumbled with her keycard and managed to unlock the door. Josh, Adam, and Miranda rushed into the corridor, their hearts pounding with relief.

As they started to go down the stairs, Josh felt a sudden blow at the back of his neck and he fell to the ground. As he struggled to stay conscious, he could hear his friend Adam being hit with a rod. Adam's screams the only thing still keeping Josh awake.

Mustering every bit of strength and resolve he had, Josh steadied himself to the point where he could see and discern what was happening. Sarah had a metal rod much akin to a baton in her hand and she was hitting Adam over the head with it. Every hit decisive; and drawing blood. She looked serious, there was a sense of calm in her demeanor and there was no hesitation in her strikes. Adam's cries for help grew weaker and weaker with every blow until a few moments later, the screams stopped. Tearing up in pain and anguish, Josh tried to get up, his head aching and groaning from pain. Unable to stand he fell back down to the floor.

Sarah walked over to him with a metal rod in her hand. "You shouldn't have come Kyano," she said, "It's too early."

Before Josh could say anything in response, she raised the rod and hit him on the side of his head, making him unconscious.

Josh's eyelids fluttered open, his vision swimming in and out of focus. A throbbing pain pulsed in his head, making him groan and clench his fists. He tried to sit up, but a wave of dizziness washed over him, forcing him back down onto the cold metal chair.

He blinked rapidly, trying to clear his vision. Slowly, the room came into focus. He was still in the torture chamber, the same sterile dark walls and flickering fluorescent bulb. But the scene before him was far more horrifying than the sterile environment.

Dominic Flyhauser and Sarah stood in front of him, their faces etched with a mixture of anger and apprehension. Dominic, his face bruised and bloodied from Josh's earlier attack, held a metal rod in his hand, its surface glinting ominously in the dim light.

Sarah, her eyes cold and calculating, held a syringe filled with a clear liquid. Her gaze flickered between Josh and Miranda, who lay slumped in a corner, her face pale and drawn. Her eyes, though filled with fear, held a flicker of defiance that mirrored Josh's own.

Next to Miranda, lay Adam, unmoving. His body was sprawled on the floor, his head tilted at an unnatural angle. A pool of blood had formed around him, staining the cold concrete floor.

The sight of his friend's lifeless body sent a jolt of terror through Josh. He let out a strangled cry, the pain in his head forgotten.

"Adam!" he screamed, his voice hoarse. "No!"

Dominic slammed his fist against the metal table, silencing Josh's cries. "Shut up!" he roared. "This is all your fault."

Josh glared at Dominic, his eyes blazing with hatred. "You killed him," he snarled. "You monster!"

Dominic sneered. "He was a nuisance," he said dismissively. "He had to be dealt with."

Sarah stepped forward, her voice calm and collected. "We can't let you leave here, Kyano," she said. "You know too much."

Josh's heart sank. He knew she was right. If they let him go, he would expose V5's secrets to the world.

"Why do you keep calling me that?" he asked, his voice trembling.

Sarah held up the syringe. "This," she said, her voice devoid of emotion. "This will silence you. And as for the name, well, let's just say that it is not your concern any longer."

Josh watched in horror as Sarah approached him, the syringe poised like a weapon. He tried to move, to fight back, but his body was weak and battered.

Just as Sarah was about to plunge the needle into his arm, he heard a voice in his head, "Call to me!" it whispered.

Confused and panicked, Josh did not know what was happening and before he could consciously understand what transpired next, he said the word, *Fury!* A flash of blinding light surrounded him and picked him up off the ground. The chair and the restraints disappeared. Sarah and

Dominic got flung away like rag dolls into the chamber walls and they slumped to the ground, watching in awe and terror, watching as Kyano took hold of his trusty partner, his first sentient weapon, the Fury.

The blue energy that covered him healed all of his wounds. It healed the pain in his head and neck and it also healed his damaged memories. The dreams he had been having of living in a fantastical world full of magical beings and powers beyond imagination, were not dreams after all, they were memories. He still had no recollection of what happened after the war and how he arrived at where he was but at the moment there was only one thing he could do.

He picked up the Fury as it pulsated with his energy. Blue specks of lightning tingling along its sharp edge and escaping as it barely held on to its rage, waiting to be unleashed.

"Give me one good reason why I shouldn't vaporize you now?" he asked, sneering at Sarah and Dominic.

The false expression of fear on their faces gave way to maniacal laughter. A cackle that deepened in tone as their bodies contorted and changed in their own right, transforming them into Raka. The mindless monsters that Kyano battled many years ago. Having fully transformed, they roared in defiance and anger as one of them lunged at Kyano. He swung his double-edged blade in a quick flurry and cleaved the Raka in two. He could now sense fear in the other monster in the room.

"You can never beat her," the Raka squealed. Its voice was just a shade louder than a hiss. "She controls reality itself!"

Kyano leapt into the air and plunged his blade into the monster's shoulder. "Tell me," He demanded, "How is it that I remember then?" and with another flourish he pushed the Fury deep into the Raka, severing its left shoulder and ending its life.

The Fury quietened down, and the whirr of energy diminished. Kyano let his blade clang to the floor and knelt down next to Miranda.

"Who are you?" she groaned, her voice still carrying hints of pain that radiated through her. Kyano called forth his blue energy and started to heal her and Adam.

"Lie still, this will take a few moments," he said reassuringly. He could feel that he did not have much energy left in him and he focused as hard as he could to try and breathe life back into Adam's body. With every passing moment he could feel his energy draining but there was no improvement in Adam. The wounds would not close. Adam was by all means dead. With what energy he could muster, he healed all of Miranda's serious injuries to a point where she could stand and walk normally. She was still covered in bruises, but Kyano could not spare any more power. He simply would not have enough energy left if there were to be another battle. The longer they took to leave V5, the higher the chances of being found. They had no idea of how many of these monsters lurked in the building and if they were disguised as humans, everyone who worked at V5 could be one of them.

Kyano moved to Adam and tried his best to do CPR but he knew, he knew in his heart that he could not bring his friend back to life. The guilt of letting Adam die was too much to bear and Kyano let out tears of anguish. The pain he felt was only compounded by the fact that he could not take more time to mourn. They had to leave. More Raka could show up at any moment and he could not afford to lose another life. He had to protect Miranda and get her to safety. With a heavy heart full of anguish and rage, Kyano stood up and helped Miranda to her feet. They had to leave immediately.

Miranda and Kyano walked out of the chamber and back into the stairwell. They climbed down the stairs and got into her car. "Drive to that apartment you sent us to," he suggested, and she followed. The drive was filled with awkward silence and glances of intrigue. Adam's loss weighed heavily on Kyano. All he could think of was the burning question of what if? If he only awakened his powers a little sooner, if the Fury had called to him a few moments sooner, he could have saved Adam. He could have saved his friend.

The Fury, lay quiet in the back seat, no noise, light or movement from it. He pondered how it was able to call to him and why he was not able to de-materialize it after. He closed his eyes and tried to concentrate, to contact his inner energy sanctum. The place in his soul, which mentored and trained him to be the warrior that he once became, but the harder he concentrated, the more frustrated he got with the endless silence in his mind that only echoed his thoughts back to him. He could not hear the voice of ethereal consciousness that was his energy. Once they reached the apartment and went inside, Miranda could not wait any longer.

"You need to start talking, Now!" she demanded. "Until yesterday, all I knew was that V5 was doing something illegal. I never in my wildest dreams imagined monsters and science fiction weapons being used, much less a person being enveloped with visible energy that can heal injuries."

Kyano slumped down to the floor. "Sit down," he said, "This is going to take some time." Telling Miranda what had happened thus far, seemed like the prudent choice. The Raka were no friends of hers, which made her an ally. He told her everything. Starting with the history of Serinia and ending with how Daryudan was defeated. As he narrated the tale, his own memories began to clear up and the haze that Hayada placed on his mind began to dissipate. By the time he was done, although he could recollect all the events, he had more questions than answers. How did Hayada do what she had done? What were her powers? And why did she alter reality this way? Why did the Fury call Kyano? How was he able to remember again?

"If I have to believe this story," Miranda interrupted, "You will only find answers if you go back to your world. Hayada is very powerful, not just as a god but also as the owner of the leading tech company of the entire world. Her influence goes past mere propaganda. She has ties in the government, in law enforcement and who knows where else. You can only defeat her if you go back and find the Scythe again. It seems like that is the only weapon that can defeat her."

"You're not wrong," Kyano replied, "Before I go, I need to know everything possible about V5. The more you can tell me about this Vbuddy earpiece, the more I will understand Hayada's purpose and her connection to this world. I need to know everything beginning with how you became involved with this."

CHAPTER

6

Clandestine Treachery

"It all started with a seemingly innocent invitation," Miranda began, her voice trembling slightly as she recounted the events that led to her capture. "A late-night meeting, a request for my expertise on a confidential project..."

Kyano listened intently, his brow furrowed in concentration. He could sense the pain and anger simmering beneath Miranda's calm exterior.

"I was flattered, of course," she continued, a bitter edge creeping into her voice. "Who wouldn't be? To be singled out by Dominic Flyhauser himself..."

She paused, her gaze fixed on the worn carpet beneath her feet. "I was naive," she whispered, more to herself than to Kyano. "I trusted them. It was too good to be true, but I trusted them. This was the big break in my career that I worked my entire life toward. This was the dream job that would settle my family and ensure that I had a worry-free rest of my life."

Miranda closed her eyes, and the scene unfolded in her mind's eye as vividly as if it were happening all over again.

It was a cold, rainy night when Miranda received the summons. A sleek, black car with tinted windows pulled up outside her apartment building, and a man in a dark suit emerged, holding an umbrella. He introduced himself as one of Dr. Flyhauser's assistants and escorted her to the waiting vehicle.

The car glided silently through the deserted streets, finally arriving at the imposing V5 headquarters. Miranda was ushered into a private elevator that ascended to the 48th floor, where Dr. Flyhauser's office was located.

The office was opulent, with floor-to-ceiling windows offering a panoramic view of the city. Dominic Flyhauser, a tall, imposing figure with a steely gaze, greeted her with a warm smile that did little to conceal the calculating glint in his eyes.

He offered her a drink, a glass of expensive scotch, and then proceeded to explain the purpose of the meeting. Dr. Flyhauser spoke of a revolutionary new project, a breakthrough in AI technology that would change the world. He needed her expertise, her unique understanding of astrophysics and quantum computing, to help refine this groundbreaking innovation.

Miranda was intrigued. She had always been fascinated by the potential of AI, and the opportunity to work on such a cutting-edge project was irresistible.

Dominic, sensing her eagerness, leaned in conspiratorially. "This is top secret, Miranda," he said, his voice low and urgent. "Lives depend on it."

Miranda felt a thrill of excitement. She was being entrusted with something truly important, something that could make a real difference in the world.

Over the next few weeks, Miranda worked tirelessly on the project, pouring all her energy and expertise into it. She met with Dominic regularly, discussing her findings and offering suggestions.

She grew to admire Dominic's brilliance and dedication. He was a visionary, a man driven by a desire to push the boundaries of what was possible. She felt honored to be working alongside him.

But as the project progressed, Miranda noticed subtle changes in Dominic's behavior. He became more secretive, more withdrawn. His smiles seemed strained; his eyes filled with a haunted look that she couldn't quite decipher.

One day, while reviewing some data, Miranda stumbled upon a disturbing anomaly. A series of code that seemed out of place, almost malicious in its intent. She brought it to Dominic's attention, her voice trembling with concern.

Dominic's reaction was swift and brutal. He accused her of insubordination, of jeopardizing the entire project. He threatened to have her removed from the team; her career ruined.

Miranda was stunned. She had never seen this side of Dominic before, this cold, ruthless persona. She tried to defend herself, to explain her concerns, but Dominic wouldn't listen.

He dismissed her, his voice laced with contempt. "You're just a physicist, Miranda," he sneered. "You don't understand the complexities of this technology."

Miranda left the meeting feeling betrayed. She couldn't shake the feeling that something was terribly wrong, that Dominic was hiding something sinister.

Her fears were confirmed a few days later when her husband, Alex, a brilliant engineer working on the same project, died suddenly in a tragic accident. The official report cited a malfunctioning piece of equipment, but Miranda couldn't help but feel that there was more to the story.

Alex had confided in her about his own concerns regarding the project, about a growing sense of unease he felt around Dominic. He had mentioned strange occurrences, unexplained glitches in the system, and a growing sense of paranoia among his colleagues.

Miranda, consumed by grief and suspicion, began her own investigation. She delved into Alex's files, searching for clues, for any indication of foul play.

What she discovered chilled her to the bone. Alex had been working on a secret project within the larger project, a fail-safe mechanism designed to prevent the AI from becoming uncontrollable. He had discovered a flaw in the system, a vulnerability that could be exploited to catastrophic effect. She found proof in Alex's files that showed that the A.I. would not be a cloud-based system as she was led to believe. The A.I had code that would enable it to read user thoughts through the earpiece, by measuring impulses. V5 was creating a closed system that would give them access to their user's most private and confidential data, their very mind.

Miranda realized that Alex had been murdered, silenced before he could expose the truth. And she knew that Dominic was responsible.

"He confessed to me in that torture chamber," Miranda said, her voice breaking. "He told me everything. He said Alex was a threat, that he had to be eliminated."

Kyano's grip tightened on the Fury. He could feel the rage building within him, a burning desire for vengeance.

Miranda continued, her voice filled with a mixture of grief and determination. "He told me about the earpiece, about its true purpose."

She explained how the earpiece was not just a communication device, but a tool of manipulation. It contained an advanced AI, Kira, that constantly monitored the user's thoughts and emotions, learning their weaknesses and vulnerabilities.

"Neural links are becoming more and more commonplace in the quantum computing world," she elaborated, "These devices enable users to control their computers by their thoughts, but the reality is that with a little manipulation of the code, these devices can become thought readers instead of simply taking instructions from their users, and that is where Kira comes in. It's not just about relaying raw data back to V5. Its about filtering them, understanding whose thoughts and which thoughts were in need of …. Intervention."

"Kira could then, in theory, influence the user's behavior, pushing them towards certain actions, manipulating their decisions, Kira could infringe upon the minds of government officials, cause wars and annihilate the entire population by just putting suggestions into key minds, it would be the end of privacy and free will!" she continued.

"It's a weapon," Miranda said, her voice filled with disgust. "A weapon designed to control and subdue the masses."

Kyano's mind reeled. He had seen the destructive power of technology firsthand, and the thought of V5 wielding such a weapon filled him with dread.

"Now it all makes sense," he said, "or at least it is starting to."

"How do you mean?" Miranda asked, puzzled.

"Hayada has the power to control reality," Kyano explained, "She can alter everyone's perception to ensure the reality of the greater populace is changed. She cannot alter the events of the past, but she can manipulate or change our memories to remember a different past so as to alter the events of the present and thereby the future."

"She was a god struck down for being a rebel," he continued, "She was castaway and imprisoned in hell because of her dangerous intentions. She wanted to control everyone's lives so that we could all live in a blissful utopia of her own making. She wanted the world to suffer less and her way of doing it was to make us all forget our sorrow and remember something else, something different. But one power she does not have is the ability to know everything. She is not omnipresent, and she cannot know everyone's thoughts and feelings. She has to be told. The gods have great power, but they are also limited by their own powers. But this Vbuddy earpiece gives her that power. If she knows what everyone thinks and feels, she can do as she pleases."

"That will be the end of the world!" Miranda cried, unable to control herself. "You have to stop her!"

"There are still a lot of questions here Miranda," Kyano replied, "We still have no idea why she is here in this world when she could have just as easily done this in mine. Whatever may be the only way for me to find out is to go home."

"And do you know how to do that?" Miranda asked questioningly.

"My dear friend Faluk opened a portal and took me through last time." Kyano recalled, "But he died in the war with Daryudan, so I have no idea how to get home."

"To add to this mystery," he continued, "In my world, I could summon my energy and do these magical things, I had an arsenal of sentient weapons that I could summon, battle with and de-materialize when I was done with them, but for some reason, after that horrid incident at V5, I am not able to talk to my inner energy like I used to. Feels like I have exhausted whatever power was left in me or ..."

"Like you have drained your battery..." Miranda interjected, "I think I know how to send you home..." she trailed off inquisitively.

Kyano's eyes widened, "How can you help?" he asked.

"If I can use whatever remaining energy, you and your weapon have, I might be able to generate a polarized energy field. I will need a plasma generator and a lot of electricity but in theory, I should be able to use your energy to send a signal to its source which in this case, I am hoping is your home world," she summarized.

"That sounds like fiction to me," Kyano said, unable to believe what he just heard.

"It's all quantum physics," she said, "A supercomputer used for classical physics stores information as a string or 0s or 1s. But a quantum computer adds an additional value called spin to each particle it studies, and this spin can be up or down or in other words a 0 or a 1. If an energy field significant enough can disrupt this flow, it can change spins by flipping them to realign with its own energy field. Or in this case, if we use your energy, it could realign spins to create an energy field that matches yours. This would mean that particles can exist as either 0 or 1 or both in a quantum energy field, they can have both upward and downward spin at the same time which means they can exist or move between two different realities. In theory, this is the basis of opening a portal to another dimension and since the energy used to open this portal is yours, the portal should open to,"

"It should open to my world," Kyano concluded.

"Now, I have no idea how much energy is required or how much you have left in you, but I know that we don't need much. Just enough to match the signature to the spin," she summarized.

"Then there is only one thing left to do," said Kyano, "We need to see my uncle and talk to him first. I owe him everything and he knows who I am. While I am away in Serinia, he can work with you to keep an eye on things here, even protect you."

"I trust you know where he lives?" Miranda said, as she stood up and grabbed her keys.

"I do," replied Kyano, "I live... lived... there too."

CHAPTER

7

The Ego of a Goddess

The sterile silence of the V5 research floor was shattered by a bloodcurdling scream. It echoed through the metallic corridors, sending shivers down the spines of even the most hardened Raka security personnel. The source of the commotion was the torture chamber, a dimly lit room reserved for the most brutal interrogations.

Jiro, one of the security guards, hurried as quickly as he could toward the room. He fumbled with his key card for a few moments but managed to open the door to the research department. He ran down the empty hallways past the deserted labs until he came upon the open door to the torture chamber at the end of the hallway. The smell was what overwhelmed his Raka senses at first. The smell of human blood and Raka blood alike that stained the floors of the most frightening chamber in the building.

Inside the chamber, a scene of utter carnage unfolded. The ominous dark walls that enclosed its prisoners in dread and inevitable fear were now splattered with blood, and the air hung heavy with the metallic tang of iron. Two Raka, who were once the head researcher and public relations officer of V5 lay sprawled on the cold metal floor, their bodies twisted in unnatural angles. Their faces were contorted in expressions of abject terror, their eyes wide with disbelief.

Jiro stumbled back against the wall, his face pale and his body trembling. This feeling was unnatural to him. As a Raka, he had the advantage of being the monster. He was the object of terror to any human who laid eyes on him. There was one occasion however, when he felt this way before. When he was filled with terror and had to run for his life. It was during the war with the Serinians. Jiro remembered the war like it happened yesterday. The vivid imagery of Layana, Merata and Kyano cleaving their way through Raka like they were fallen leaves on the ground. The imagery of other Raka falling prey to the warrior's every slash and thrust. There was only one possible explanation for what he was witnessing. One of the warriors of light had been there.

He knew he had to report this to the CEO of V5. He had to tell, '*her*' and the thought of facing her filled him with dread. With sweaty palms and a cold shiver running down his spine, he made his way to the private elevator located at the other end of the research floor. Tapping his key card, he entered and pressed the button to the penthouse office. When he arrived, he heard the familiar voice of Kira, the V5 A.I over the intercom on the elevator before the doors opened.

"Welcome to the penthouse office suite," it said in a robotic monotone, "Madam CEO is in residence and available to meet with you presently. Please state your name and the purpose of your visit so I may appraise her."

"My name is Jiro, security guard number 08764. I came to report on an incident that happened on the research floor," he said in as calm a voice as he could muster. A brief period of silence ensued which did not do anything to quell Jiro's anxiety.

The elevator doors then opened slowly as Kira spoke again, "Welcome to the office of the CEO."

The office was a reflection of her personality: cold, austere, and intimidating. The walls were painted a stark white, and the only furniture was a massive mahogany desk and a plush leather armchair that was facing the window. The bookshelves that lined the office walls were filled with old texts and books that seemed were not from this world. The private collection of knowledge that in itself contained many secrets of life, death and of existence itself.

As Jiro entered, he could hear the cackle of the fireplace burning away in the corner. The pleasant piano music that played in the background only added to the eeriness of the encounter. As he looked around carefully, he heard her voice from behind the desk.

"Jiro," Hayada said in a voice that was as sharp as a knife. "I hear there has been an incident in the torture chamber."

Jiro swallowed hard and nodded. "Yes, your excellency. There... there have been a couple of deaths, both Raka."

Hayada's eyes narrowed. "Dead? How?"

Jiro stammered, struggling to find the words to describe what he had seen. "They were... they were killed by... by a warrior of light."

Hayada spun around in her chair, her gaze fixed on Jiro. "A warrior of light?" she repeated, her voice dripping with skepticism. "Are you sure you know what you saw, Jiro?"

Jiro met her gaze, his voice trembling with conviction. "Yes, your highness. I am sure. I saw Dominic and Sarah's bodies. They were both cleaved into pieces."

Hayada's expression softened slightly. "Very well," she said. "Tell me everything."

Jiro poured out his story, describing the torture chamber as he saw it. He described the fear he felt and how akin it was to the last time he felt such terror. The Raka had bodies hardened by dark energy. To the layman, their bodies were harder than steel and it would require the force of a wrecking ball concentrated on the edge of a sword to cause this kind of damage. That kind of power was alien to this world. That kind of power had to be from the other side of the mirror.

When Jiro finished, Hayada remained silent for a long moment. Then, she spoke, her voice low and dangerous.

"This, changes everything," she said. "We must find who did this and eliminate them!"

Hayada's eyes blazed with a cold fire, and Jiro knew that she would not rest until she found the ones responsible. He knew that he was lucky to have escaped with his life, and he vowed to do everything in his power to assist Hayada in her mission.

"Go," Hayada said, dismissing Jiro with a wave of her hand. "I have much to think about."

As Jiro left the room, Hayada's thoughts turned to Kyano. She had underestimated him. She had thought that by erasing his memories, she had neutralized him. But she had been wrong.

Kyano was a threat, a loose end that needed to be tied up. She had to find him and kill him this time. She was not going to take the risk of leaving him alive again. As amusing as it was to cause the warriors of light, her beloved father's pets unexpected grief, she decided not to underestimate their resilience anymore.

Hayada's eyes narrowed, and a cold smile played on her lips. As she considered her next moves, she recollected the vast history of her own life. The history of what led to the current circumstances.

CHAPTER

8

A Dark Point of View

The fires of Hell raged around her, a symphony of torment and despair. Hayada, the fallen goddess, stood amidst the inferno, her once radiant form now shrouded in shadows. Her eyes, once filled with the light of creation, now burned with a cold, malevolent fire.

Millennia had passed since she had been cast out of the heavens, condemned for her hubris and her insatiable thirst for power. She had dared to challenge the balance of life and death, to manipulate the very fabric of reality. The other gods, fearing her unchecked power, had stripped her of her divinity and imprisoned her in this infernal abyss.

But Hayada was not one to be easily subdued. She seethed with resentment, her heart consumed by a burning desire for revenge. She would not rest until she had reclaimed her rightful place and overthrown those who had wronged her.

As eons passed, Hayada's rage festered, twisting her once noble spirit into something dark and twisted. She delved into the forbidden arts, mastering the arcane secrets of necromancy and the manipulation of souls. She learned to harness the very essence of fear and despair, twisting it to her will.

One day, within the depths of Hell, she felt a kindred presence from the mortal realm. Daryudan, the fallen knight of Serinia, the warrior who was wronged by his own king, betrayed by the very kingdom he protected. She reached out to him and made the dreaded pact. She granted limitless power to Daryudan in exchange for his commitment to inflict unending torment and suffering upon the humans of Serinia. Being manipulative was in her very core. Her very nature was to control, to contort but also to seek pleasure in the outcome of her own actions. Her father, the almighty Dimarius decreed that Hayada would be free of her prison on such a day as when his Scythe was used to reap evil from the mortal world. That was her chance. That was why Daryudan received the bounty of dark power that he did. For he was so powerful that there was only one weapon that could defeat him, the Scythe of Serinia.

Unbeknownst to this ulterior agenda, Daryudan would wage war on the mortal realm, spreading chaos and destruction, while Hayada would manipulate him and his actions from the shadows, subtly tilting the balance in their favor, waiting for Dimarius to make the next move. Daryudan's armies swept across the land, leaving a trail of death and devastation in their wake.

But Hayada's true goal was not merely to conquer the mortal realm. She sought to control the very essence of life and death, to become the arbiter of fate itself. She believed that with enough power, she could rewrite reality, reshape the world in her own image.

As the final battle raged, Hayada watched from the shadows, her heart filled with anticipation. She saw Kyano, the warrior prince, emerge as a beacon of hope, alongside his sister Layana and their dear friend Merata, slicing through Daryudan's forces like a whirlwind.

A cold smile spread across Hayada's lips. The warriors of light had the Scythe in their hands. She watched gleefully as Kyano hoodwinked Daryudan. His plan and the use of Layans' cloaking magic to conceal the Scythe in Merata's hand did the trick. They knew Daryudan would target Merata as she was the newest warrior of light and whom he considered to be a weak link. His thoughts would be to kill her and when

Kyano and Layana are caught off guard by Merata's death, he would finish them as well. When Daryudan rushed at Merata, as predicted, Kyano put their plan into motion. They used Layan's cloaking magic to give Merata the Scythe. The Scythe which Daryudan could not see until he was lunging at Merata with his Halberd raised above head. Daryudan, clearly caught by surprise, had little chance of avoiding the hit. He quickly put his left hand to his back and drew the shield that Hayada gave him. The shield that he was told would block an attack from the Scythe. He shifted his position mid-air as he got closer to Merata, shield at the front and halberd raised in his right hand.

Merata crouched low and swung around with all her might. The Scythe contacted the shield and went straight through it. Straight through, all the way through Daryudan and out of his back. Before Merata even had a chance to think, her assassin instincts took over and as she spun through the attack that she unleashed with the Scythe, she plunged Assylia, into Daryudan's side. The Scythe stripped Daryudan of his immortality and Assylia, the sentient weapon of poison moved its power swiftly through Daryudan's body. He sank to the ground, unable to bear the pain. He took a hold of the blade sticking to his side and yanked it out, blood spewing from the wound. The poison took hold of him and his skin began to go pale. As he lay there in what would be his final moments, all he could think of was the weight of betrayal that he now felt. The shield that Hayada promised would protect him, did nothing at all. She betrayed Daryudan and left him to die. Before he could ponder why this happened to him, he began to choke on his own blood and shortly after, he stopped moving.

The demon was dead.

When Daryudan fell, Hayada seized her opportunity. She reached into Kyano's mind, subtly altering his memories, erasing his past, and implanting false narratives. She twisted his perception of reality, making him believe that he was merely a human, a soldier fighting for a cause he no longer remembered.

She took him with her across the mirror and implanted him back into his old life. Into the life he lived as a blissful young man, growing up with his photographer uncle and wanting to do nothing more than graduate from college and become a journalist. There had to be balance and she needed a place to weave her intricate plan away from the influence of all the other meddling gods. Just as there is light and its opposite, darkness, just as there was life with its reflection being death, there were two realities. An inevitability of alternate existence which was a direct result of her father, Dimarius's creation.

The cackle of the fireplace diverted her attention for a moment and Hayada stared into the fire. She watched as the flames danced as they engulfed the very wood, the very fuel that gave them life. They burned bright and glorious, all the while not knowing that their actions would be the very reason they would extinguish themselves. Much like the gods who were ignorant or perhaps just in denial of the consequence of their own, inaction.

Hayada could never understand why the other gods sought to let live rather than control those who worshipped them. But then again, the other gods did not understand her point of view. Her endless questions often met with disbelief or at best irritation, but she knew that she was far more intelligent and aware. She knew the truth, just like her brothers and sisters did. The truth of the universe, of life and death, the truth of time, the ultimate and the only truth of existence itself. The truth that time was not a straight line. It was a circle. A perfect circle of infinite radius that kept marching on itself both forwards and backwards. What once was would be once more and what is to come had already happened. Around this circle of time danced the two serpents of creation. The golden serpent of life and the black serpent of death. The two intertwined in a helix around the line of time that formed the circumference of the entire sphere of existence. The time that is now passing was at the very forefront, the tips of the heads of both serpents and their consistent struggle for dominance over each other led the flow of time.

In this never-ending war, the battles won by life would see prosperity in existence whereas the battles won by death would see despair. The god of existence, Dimarius and his entire horde of lower gods were simply spectators, guardians that kept both life and death in check. They knew when light would triumph over darkness, and they knew when darkness would overpower light. They could see it all coming on the line of time. As could Hayada. When she matured and saw what her role as a god would be, she could not accept it. She could not simply say, '*Yes father, I will do as I am told,*' She could not acquiesce. For she had the power to manipulate reality. The perception of what was and the consciousness of what is were under her authority. She could not alter events that occurred for she could not move time backwards, but she could make any mortal think that those events did not happen. In doing so, she could alter the course of what was to come.

Dimarius created the world of Serinia when the line of time dictated for him to do so and in doing so, gave rise to the universe in which lay Earth. There can be no opaque object without a shadow. Everything the gods did as was written in the line of time had opposite consequences. A universe ruled by gods thus had an equivalent that existed with no gods. Such was the balance dictated by time.

Hayada also felt that the other gods were no more than hypocrites. They cited the rules of time when it suited their needs and yet still meddled in the mortal realm when it was to their fancy. They were all interested in progressing life and light instead of controlling the balance as they were supposed to do. This was always too much for her to bear. She could see the power she had, the power that the other gods had being squandered to the whims of Dimarius as he willfully ignored his duties and so she rebelled.

As Hayada sat in her office contemplating these thoughts, she vividly recollected the incident when she was cast out. The incident that happened all those eons ago that started the journey that led her here today.

She had decided to steal the Scythe of Serinia. The most powerful weapon in all of existence. Her powers of altering reality were limited to mortals. She could not alter the fates of gods or any being that lived outside of the mortal realm. But with the Scythe, she could bend them to her will. She could show them how to truly be gods and rule the universe the way it was meant to be ruled. She would threaten them if she had to. With the gods under her thumb, she could then finally control the circle of time and the infinite cycle of life and death. That, in her mind, was what it meant to be a god. To have absolute and complete control over everything. There was no meaning, no point to existence if time was simply a circle that kept repeating itself. It needed to flow forwards, not back. It needed to move ahead and pave the way for new creation, for different existence, to proliferate not to encapsulate.

She snuck into Dimarius's chamber as quietly as she could. She knew her father was occupied elsewhere and that he would not be disturbed by anything until he was done. She saw the Scythe sitting atop its silver mantle and walked as quickly and quietly as she could. As she held out her hand to take hold of it, a force like nothing she ever felt repelled her. She was thrown ten feet in the air and twice as far and landed with a thud across the chamber. Gathering her wits, she stood up to see her father, Dimarius, his eyes colored gold, Scythe held high. It only made sense to her then that the most powerful sentient weapon would have a mind of its own and would not go willingly and her father would not let her simply steal his weapon.

"You have crossed the line, daughter," he sneered, "You will pay for this."

"Oh please father," she retorted, "You sit here in your endless palace of glory and infinite luxury as the mortal world below suffers and rejoices in an endless cycle of torment and pleasure. We need to break the cycle and usher a new dawn of existence."

"You know not what you speak of Hayada," Dimarius recanted, "The forces you meddle with are beyond your control. They are beyond even

Gods. Why do you think there is a new God born every cycle? It is so we can keep the peace!"

"And for every new God, there is yet a new Demon born just the same," Hayada retaliated, "With the same vigor and the same power, only dark, a stark opposite to your light to wreak havoc unchecked! What you and the others are letting happen is eventuality. The final war of all wars. I have seen it on the line of time. The point in time beyond which our vision ceases to see. The point at which it all ends in a spectacular war that engulfs all, gods, demons, mortals, there will be nothing left, not even time."

"Enough of your insolence!" screamed Dimarius, "The order of existence is not to be questioned and for what you have on your poisonous mind, you can spend eternity contemplating it in the netherworld."

"Accurse amigla!" screamed Dimarius and brought forth the light of judgement from the Scythe. In a flash, dark menacing chains appeared around Hayada's wrists and locked her inside a cage made of the same darkness. She pleaded to her father with her eyes and for an instant, just an instant, he hesitated. She then disappeared from his presence and was banished to the netherworld.

Dimarius sat down on his throne and cried that day. He had to do the deed, but the loss of his daughter was too great. He had to teach her a lesson, but the pain of her punishment was too much. He had to make a way for her to be free again, but only if she was to learn the error of her ways. As he stared at his Scythe, it was then that he decided, and his decision was decreed. When evil is so powerful in the mortal world that the Scythe must be used to defeat it, Hayada will have had no choice but to accept that the balance of time is what enables creation to exist. Then she is granted freedom from the netherworld but can never step foot in the world of the gods.

Her trusty fireplace snapped her thoughts back to her office. The patter of heavy rain outside foretold events that would unfold. She knew Kyano would not go quietly. She suspected that he would do everything he could to make his way back to Serinia. To the one place where he could get reinforcements to attack her stronghold. He was powerful enough to defeat any Raka, any monster she could throw at him. She knew that it was time to visit the netherworld and have a chat with her old friend. Perhaps he would be kind enough to help her once again. Perhaps she could use him one more time to further her plans. She was going to see Daryudan.

CHAPTER

9

The Soldier, the Prince and the Wildcard

The quiet suburban street was a stark contrast to the turmoil brewing inside Kyano. He gripped the steering wheel, his knuckles white, as he navigated the familiar route to his uncle Jeremiah's house. Beside him, Miranda sat in tense silence, her gaze fixed on the passing scenery, her mind awhirl with the enormity of their mission.

Kyano pulled up to the curb, the quaint two-story house a beacon of normalcy in a world that had suddenly turned upside down. He cut the engine, the silence amplifying the pounding of his heart.

"Ready?" Miranda asked, her voice soft.

Kyano took a deep breath, steeling himself for the conversation ahead. "As I'll ever be," he replied, a wry smile tugging at his lips.

They stepped out of the car and walked towards the house, their footsteps crunching on the gravel driveway. Kyano reached for the doorbell, his finger hovering over the button. He hesitated, a wave of uncertainty washing over him. How would Jeremiah react to this news? Would he believe them? Would he understand?

He pressed the button, the familiar chime echoing through the house. A moment later, the door swung open, revealing Jeremiah's smiling face.

"Josh!" he exclaimed, his eyes widening in surprise. "You brought a friend! What a pleasant surprise! Come in, come in."

"Hey Uncle Jer, this is Miranda," Kyano introduced. His expression struggling to stay calm but still belying his intentions.

They stepped into the warm, inviting living room, the scent of freshly brewed coffee filling the air. Jeremiah gestured towards the couch, and they settled in, the soft cushions sinking beneath their weight.

"So, what brings you two here?" Jeremiah asked, his eyes twinkling with curiosity.

Kyano exchanged a glance with Miranda. It was time to tell him everything.

He began with the voicemail, the mysterious message that had set them on this path. He described their encounter with Sarah, the unsettling tour of V5 headquarters, and the discovery of the thumb drive with Miranda's video. He recounted the horrors Miranda had witnessed, the torture chamber, the missing employees, the chilling truth about V5's sinister agenda.

Jeremiah listened intently, his expression shifting from curiosity to concern to disbelief. When Kyano finished, a heavy silence settled over the room.

"I... I don't know what to say," Jeremiah finally stammered, his voice laced with shock. "This is... unbelievable."

"I know it's a lot to take in," Miranda said gently. "But it's the truth."

"I remember now," Kyano added, his gaze fixed on his uncle's eyes, "I am Kyano of Serin."

Jeremiah looked at them, his eyes searching theirs. He saw the fear, the determination, the unwavering conviction in their voices. Kyano's words hanging in his ears, echoing and lifting the burden of the false life he was living.

He knelt on one knee and raised his right hand to his shoulder, "I am here to serve your highness!"

"Get up uncle," Kyano said, holding Jeremiah's shoulders, "You raised me! You never have to stand on ceremony with me. You will always be family." The two men hugged, their emotions rushing and relief billowing in their minds.

"I am glad you remember where we came from," continued Kyano, "It will make explaining what you forgot that much easier."

Kyano then went on to tell Jeremiah about how Faluk and Saldah came to their home and took them to Serin and the events that followed. He spoke about meeting his father, the king of Serin, and how Daryudan used him as a spy. About meeting his long-lost sister Layana, who was condemned to death but saved by Faluk and raised in secrecy unbeknownst to the king and Queen. He spoke about the three battles he fought in, the weapons he mastered and ultimately about Daryudan's demise and Hayada's cunning.

Jeremiah listened in shock and awe. Mere words, not doing justice to his absent memories. Although he couldn't quite grasp the full gravity of the events that he forgot had happened, he knew enough to trust the details his nephew shared. He was overcome with emotions of grief at the loss of the king, the fall of Serin but also relief and joy at Daryudan's defeat. He understood the heavy toll the mortal realm had to pay to rid itself of Daryudan's menace. His mind grew fierce with resolve. He wanted to do something. He had to help fight this unbeatable god because if anything, Serinians never gave up. They never stopped fighting.

"So, what are you going to do?" Jeremiah asked, his voice still shaky but resolute.

"We're going to stop them," Kyano said, his voice firm. "We're going to expose V5 and bring that company down."

"I assume you also considered the fact that V5 is run by the most hated and most feared goddess of all Serinia," Jeremiah replied, his sarcasm subtle yet exuding confidence.

Jeremiah added slowly. "I believe you," he said. "And I want to help."

Kyano and Miranda looked at him, surprised. "You do?" Miranda asked.

"Knowing what I know now, I cannot just sit here and let you both have all the fun," Jeremiah retorted, "I cannot let Hayada get away with this."

"And we need your help," Kyano said, "But not to fight. I need you here, on earth, to work with Miranda while I am away. I need you to keep an eye on V5 so that when I return with our friends, you will have a strategy that we can execute. A plan to defeat Hayada forever."

"What are you hoping to gain by going to Serinia?" asked a defeated Jeremiah, "Warriors of light you may be, but Layana, Merata and you cannot defeat a god!"

"I am going to find the Scythe again," Kyano replied, determination screaming in his voice, "I will bring it here and I will end her life! Now if you are satisfied with my answer, can we please plan on how to get our hands on some specific equipment!"

Jeremiah gave him a quick nod and they all sat down at the dinner table to discuss their next steps. Miranda spoke about a plasma generator at the University that they could use to open the portal.

"The university?" questioned Kyano, "Really?"

"Yes," replied Miranda, "When I was doing my graduate studies in quantum computing, the particle physics department used to collaborate with us on a few projects. They have a plasma generator that we can use."

"I hope you're right," replied Kyano not making any effort to hide his skepticism.

"Look, I understand this sounds crazy," Miranda said, a hint of defensiveness creeping into her voice. "But trust me, this is our best shot. The plasma generator creates a concentrated energy field, and with the Fury..."

"It could amplify the energy field enough to open a portal," Jeremiah finished her sentence, a flicker of understanding in his eyes.

Kyano, finally beholding a working plan, ran a hand through his hair, the memories of Serinia – vivid and compelling – flashing before him like a fragmented dream. "Okay," he said, a newfound resolve hardening his gaze. "Let's do this."

Jeremiah, with his knowledge of technology and his connections in the city, proved to be an invaluable resource. He helped them refine their strategy, offering suggestions and insights they hadn't considered.

As the conversation drew to a close, Jeremiah's expression turned serious. "Be careful," he warned. "V5 is powerful. They won't hesitate to silence anyone who threatens their plans."

Kyano nodded. "We know. But we have to do this."

Jeremiah smiled. "I know you do. And I'm proud of you both."

He embraced them both in a warm hug, a silent promise of support and solidarity. As they pulled away, he reached into his pocket and pulled out a small, intricately carved wooden box.

"This is for you, Kyano," he said, handing him the box. "It's something I've been saving for a special occasion."

Kyano opened the box, his eyes widening in surprise. Inside, nestled on a bed of velvet, was a gleaming silver dagger, its blade etched with ancient runes.

"It's beautiful," Kyano whispered, his fingers tracing the intricate patterns.

"It's more than just beautiful," Jeremiah said. "It's a weapon, forged by the finest craftsmen in Serinia. It's said to be imbued with protective magic."

Kyano looked at him, his heart swelling with gratitude. "Thank you, Jeremiah," he said. "I won't let you down."

They left Jeremiah's house with a renewed sense of purpose, armed with a weapon and a promise of support. They knew the road ahead would be dangerous, but they were ready to face whatever challenges awaited them. They had a world to save.

The drive to the university was tense, the silence punctuated only by the hum of the engine and the rhythmic swish of the windshield wipers battling the persistent drizzle. Kyano gripped the Fury, the cool metal a comforting weight in his hand. He still couldn't quite grasp the reality of his situation – one minute he was a budding journalist, the next he was a warrior prince tasked with saving a world he forgot he remembered.

Miranda pulled up to the loading dock behind the physics department, the familiar brick facade looming in the twilight. "This is it," she said, her voice barely above a whisper. "Remember the plan?"

Kyano nodded. "You create a diversion; I knock out the guard and we take his key card."

Miranda gave him a quick, reassuring smile. "Be careful."

"Wait," Kyano said, "You have to be careful once I leave. Stay away from V5."

"You don't have to worry about me," Miranda said, "I can take care of myself."

"Even so," Kyano continued, "Be careful!"

"Thank you," Miranda replied.

She stepped out of the car, her heels clicking on the wet asphalt. Kyano watched as she approached the security guard stationed at the entrance, her confident stride and disarming smile a stark contrast to the turmoil brewing inside him.

He waited for his cue, his heart pounding in his chest. He could hear the faint sounds of Miranda's conversation with the guard, her voice rising in mock outrage. He watched as she pulled down the garbage bin while the guard was distracted. That was his cue. The falling garbage bin made a clatter and spewed its contents onto the ground, prompting the guard to try and clean it up as best he could.

Kyano slipped out of the car and darted towards Miranda and the guard. With a swift flourish of his hand, he knocked the unsuspecting guard unconscious. Miranda then quickly took the guard's key card and they both ran to the door. They navigated the maze of corridors, Kyano following Miranda the whole way. The air was thick with the smell of ozone and burnt metal, a familiar scent from his time in Serinia.

They reached the lab where the plasma generator was housed. The door was locked, but Kyano, with a surge of newfound strength, simply kicked it open. The hinges splintered, and the door crashed inward.

The generator sat in the center of the room, a hulking mass of wires and coils, humming with barely contained energy. Kyano approached it cautiously, his eyes scanning the complex control panel. He had no idea how to operate this thing. Miranda quickly went to the control chamber in the corner of the room which had the power switch. She fumbled around with the key card doing her best to get the door to open quickly. They did not have much time.

Just then, they heard footsteps approaching. Kyano spun around, the Fury gripped tightly in his hand. Two security guards burst into the room; their faces contorted with anger.

"Hold it right there!" one of them shouted, his hand reaching for his taser.

Kyano didn't hesitate. He lunged forward, the Fury slicing through the air with a whoosh. Kyano turned the blade backwards so he wouldn't mortally injure the guards who were simply doing their jobs. The guards cried out in surprise, their tasers clattering to the floor. Kyano pressed his advantage, his movements fluid and precise. He disarmed the guards with a swift kick, sending them sprawling to the ground.

He turned back to the generator, his heart pounding. He had to get this thing working. He closed his eyes, focusing on the energy within him, the power of the Scythe thrumming in his veins. Miranda managed to get the control chamber opened and flicked the big red lever to turn the power on.

Suddenly, the generator sprang to life, its hum intensifying into a roar. Arcs of electricity crackled and snaked across the surface, illuminating the room in a blinding blue light. Kyano stumbled back, shielding his eyes.

Now, he just needed to create the portal.

He gripped the Fury tightly, channeling his energy into the blade. He raised his double-edged sword, its deep crimson surface shimmering with power. He brought it down towards the generator, the metal screeching in protest.

A blinding flash of light erupted, and a wave of energy pulsed outwards, throwing Kyano back against the wall. He gasped for breath, his vision blurred. Gathering himself as quickly as he could, he stood up again, then he saw it.

A swirling vortex of energy, shimmering and pulsating in the center of the room. The portal.

He had done it. He had opened a gateway to Serinia.

He took a step towards the portal, his heart pounding with a mixture of fear and anticipation. He could feel the pull of Serinia, the call of his destiny.

He turned back to look at Miranda, who stood frozen in the control chamber, her eyes wide with awe. He gave her a reassuring nod.

"I'll be back," he said, his voice filled with a newfound confidence.

Then, he stepped into the portal, disappearing into the swirling vortex of energy.

The portal collapsed behind him, the light fading, the hum of the generator dying down. Miranda stood there for a moment, the silence pressing in on her. Then, she let out a shaky breath.

Kyano was gone. He was back in Serinia, where he belonged.

She had done her part. Now, it was up to him to save the world.

CHAPTER

10

Warcry

The air crackled with malevolent energy as Hayada descended into the Netherworld. Sulfurous fumes choked her lungs, and the oppressive heat pressed down like a physical weight. Jagged obsidian spires pierced the crimson sky, casting long, menacing shadows across the desolate landscape. Rivers of fire snaked through the scorched earth, their molten currents illuminating the tortured souls trapped within.

Hayada descended slowly, with the grace of a feather falling to the ground on a windless morn. Her steps barely made a noise as she landed. Elegance was becoming of the dark goddess. She strode along a long and winding path that carved a molten river into two. Screams and moans echoed all around her from voices that held no presence. Fire and brimstone spewed out of the river as it bubbled endlessly with the prominence of a star. It never cooled down, it never changed. A deranged creature, struggling to catch its breath, black in its entirety, with the form of a man, pulled itself out of the river. Screeching and scorching, it started to cool down and lay on the banks, heaving, catching its breath. Its body started to harden to black charcoal. The creature, now looked more like a man. He started to clear the charcoal off of his face and body and picked himself up. Crawling and still struggling to breathe he made his way to the top of the bank and on to the pathway that Hayada was on. He crept up to her and lay on the ground, his breathing starting to get more even.

With a little smirk, Hayada waved her hand, and the man was enveloped in black energy. It picked him up off the ground and flew him away. In the heart of this infernal realm stood a fortress of obsidian and bone, its imposing silhouette a testament to Hayada's twisted genius. This was no ordinary prison; it was a repository of vengeance, a carefully curated collection of souls Hayada had encountered throughout the millennia. Each prisoner, a vessel of raw, untamed wrath, fueled by an insatiable thirst for retribution. Just as Hayada had done all through her imprisonment, she added, yet another soul to her collection, the man covered in smoldering ash and charcoal.

Hayada had long foreseen a potential conflict with the other gods, a clash of wills that could only end one way. A war between gods and demons to overthrow the narrow minded and egomaniacal Dimarius. These imprisoned souls, she believed, would be her ultimate weapon, her heralds of darkness unleashed to wreak havoc upon those who had wronged her.

Hayada was careful and planned everything down to the last excruciating detail. To that end, she had also forged weapons to give to her army when the time arose. Weapons… Dark weapons… imbued with dark energy, the energy of death. For eons, Dimarius and the other gods had taught and preached the ways of creation and life and what it meant when a life ended. In their minds the distinction of life and death was merely life and the absence of life. But Hayada, now, knew different. Her isolation in the netherworld taught her a great many things but the first lesson that she learnt, the hidden truth of existence that opened her eyes was that death was not the absence of life. It was a transitioned form of life.

Dead souls travelled to the netherworld and suffered endlessly for what sins they committed while alive. These souls were merely apparitions, even here in this place of desolation. Wisps of energy, remnants of a once living consciousness that was doomed to a fate of torture and punishment. Once in a decade or so, however, in the netherworld, a doomed soul would find the most elusive thing in death… resolve. To be someone again, to be whole again. These marked souls would take form if they could endure the torture the netherworld had to offer and come out of it stronger. They would take shape and regain a body similar to the one they had in life. Overcoming a gruesome ordeal such as that and finding a magnificent reward could only do one thing to that mind and that was to fill it with thoughts of retribution and desire for vengeance. When Hayada saw these creatures, she had realized that the gods had been wrong and then a mutinous thought crept into her mind. A thought so poisonous that it was simply too irresistible for Hayada. These necro warriors as Hayada liked to call them could be her army. If she could escape the netherworld, she would then have the power to traverse freely between the realms of life and death. She could lead her undead warriors of darkness out of this realm and back to the very reality that killed them, to wreak havoc once more. Only this time, they would have powerful weapons and a goddess for a warlord.

With a wave of her hand, Hayada summoned a portal, its swirling vortex leading to the depths of her fortress. She stepped through, the oppressive heat intensifying as she descended into the labyrinthine corridors. Tormented screams echoed through the stone passageways, a chilling reminder of the suffering she held captive within these walls. Souls that regained their bodies needed time to adjust and gain the idea of thought and speech. These souls and thier bodies weren't birthed. They weren't made and they certainly weren't nurtured or nourished by the loving hands of a doting parent. They clawed and fought their way to be a semblance of their lost life and this took a lot of time and endurance. Usually, when they first manifest, these necro warriors were full of anger. Their minds twisted and contorted by madness and pain. Hayada's fortress was a place that conditioned them. That gave them time to overcome their mental anguish and regain consciousness.

Finally, she reached Daryudan's cell. The heavy iron door, etched with runes of binding and suppression, creaked open, revealing an opulent chamber bathed in an eerie, ethereal glow. A throne of dragon bone dominated the center of the room, and shadowy figures flitted about, attending to every whim of the warlord seated upon it.

Daryudan's eyes snapped open, his gaze locking onto Hayada with a fury that could ignite the very air. His face, contorted by the condition that afflicted him, death. His pallor and grotesque façade a mere shadow of his former self, he looked very much *undead*. "You!" he snarled, his voice a guttural growl that echoed through the chamber. "You dare show your face after your treachery?"

He rose from his throne, his imposing figure radiating an aura of power and rage. "You promised me victory, you promised me glory!" he roared, his voice laced with the bitterness of betrayal. "Instead, you used me, manipulated me, cast me aside like a broken toy!" He then manifested a spear of energy, spewing its purple guts from its edges. Without hesitation he flung the weapon at Hayada. The goddess dismissed the energy spear like it was nothing. She didn't flinch or even raise a hand. The weapon simply disintegrated as it got close to her.

"Is this what you have become now?" she questioned, sarcasm apparent in her voice, "A spoilt brat who throws tantrums because he didn't understand a decision made for his own good?"

Daryudan screamed in rage and threw ten more spears at Hayada, each spear more powerful than the last and each throw harder and faster than before and each spear met the same fate. They all fell into nothingness a few feet from their intended target. Hayada had already spoken. She asked him a question. Regardless of how her decision to let him die was perceived by him, as far as she was concerned, he was still one of her warriors and she was still his master. Daryudan needed to respect that. She was willing to be patient and let his rage burn out, but she would not stand to let him insult her. She would not utter another word and stood there, her gaze beckoning him to use his words like a civilized adult.

He paced before her, his every step reverberating with barely contained fury. "You robbed me of my triumph, of my rightful place as ruler of Serinia!" he spat. "You turned me into a martyr for your own twisted ambitions!"

Hayada met his gaze, her expression unwavering. "Your destiny was never merely to conquer mortals, Daryudan," she said, her voice calm and measured. "You were meant for greater things." Her tone, somber yet assertive, made Daryudan pause his incessant pacing and listen. Somewhere in the depths of his sub consciousness, he was still obeying Hayada of his own free will and she could sense that.

She gestured towards the shadowy figures attending him. "I have not abandoned you either. You live a lavish life in a world of torture and terror because I have decreed so. With just cause as a reward for your services. I gave you this gift and many others, Daryudan because there is a greater calling that I am going to entrust you with. I have done what I have done so I could prepare you."

"Prepare me for what?" he scoffed. "To rot in this gilded cage?"

"To wage war against the gods themselves," Hayada declared, her eyes gleaming with a fierce intensity.

She stepped closer, her voice dropping to a conspiratorial whisper. "The universe is trapped in an endless cycle, Daryudan, a repetitive dance of creation and destruction. The two serpents, Life and Death, eternally entwined, their struggle dictating the flow of time. Dimarius and his minions protect and oversee this cycle, paying no heed to what happens to the lives they create to populate this meaningless existence. Such are the gods that mortals worship and admire. The line of time flows in a cycle and history will repeat itself. In different circumstances and with different hands at the helm of each prominent junction but still, history will repeat itself. Light triumphs over darkness and yet, darkness wins over light and the cycle continues."

"And you believe you can break this cycle?" Daryudan challenged, his voice laced with skepticism.

"I will not break it," Hayada corrected, her voice ringing with conviction. "I will obliterate it and pave the way for a new reality, free from this prison of nonsense. I will create paradise!"

She looked at Daryudan, her eyes burning with a messianic zeal. "Join me, Daryudan. Together, we will rewrite the rules of existence, usher in an era of true peace, an era where the endless conflict between good and evil finally ceases."

She extended her hand, offering him a partnership, a chance to transcend his mortal limitations and become something more. "Together, we will reshape the universe."

Daryudan stared at Hayada's outstretched hand, his face a mask of conflicting emotions. The fires of his rage still flickered within him, but a spark of curiosity, a flicker of something akin to hope, ignited in their depths.

"Reshape the universe?" he echoed, his voice low and thoughtful. "A universe without this endless cycle of conflict? A universe where good does not inevitably triumph over evil, only to be overthrown in turn?"

He looked at Hayada, his eyes searching hers for any hint of deceit, any flicker of the manipulation he had come to expect. But all he saw was a burning conviction, a fierce determination that mirrored his own.

"Tell me more," he said, his voice gruff but laced with a newfound curiosity.

Hayada smiled, a slow, predatory curve formed on her lips. "The gods are content to play their games, Daryudan," she explained, her voice smooth as silk. "They watch from their lofty perches, manipulating events, choosing champions, all while claiming to uphold some grand cosmic balance."

"But what is balance?" she challenged, her voice rising in intensity. "Is it merely an endless tug-of-war between opposing forces, a never-ending cycle of victory and defeat? Or is true balance something more, something beyond this petty struggle?"

She stepped closer, her eyes locking with his. "I believe there is a different path, Daryudan. A path where the serpents of Life and Death do not merely dance around the circle of time, but merge, intertwine, become one."

She held his gaze, her voice laced with exuberance, "Imagine a universe where life and death are not opposing forces, but two sides of the same coin. A universe where creation and destruction exist in perfect harmony, where the flow of time is not a circle, but a spiral, ever ascending, ever evolving."

Daryudan felt a shiver run down his spine. This vision, this radical departure from the established order, resonated with a deep longing within him. He had always chafed against the constraints of destiny, the predetermined roles assigned to him and his kind.

"And what part do you see me playing in this grand scheme?" he asked, his voice laced with cautious skepticism.

Hayada's smile widened, revealing a hint of sharp teeth. "You, Daryudan, are the catalyst. You are the one who will break the chains of fate, shatter the old order, and pave the way for a new era."

She placed her hand on his arm, her touch surprisingly gentle. "Imagine fighting by my side, Daryudan. We would be unstoppable. You would be my right hand, the very weapon I wield to vanquish those who stand in front of me and pave the way for a reality that no god has seen before."

Daryudan's eyes widened in revelation. A chance to go back to the mortal realm beckoned him. A chance to once more be free and wreak havoc on the humans that wronged him, a task he relished above all else.

"Alright," he replied, "I will pledge my blade to you, Hayada, goddess of the netherworld. I will usher in a new reality, one that will be the envy of every god who decided to wrong you, a reality that never happened before!"

CHAPTER

11

Despair and Determination

Kyano blinked, his eyes struggling to adjust to the oppressive darkness. A wave of dizziness washed over him, and he stumbled, his hand instinctively reaching out to steady himself. The rough texture of cold stone met his fingertips, grounding him in the unsettling reality of his surroundings.

He was no longer in the steam punk, wired madness of the university physics lab. This place felt ancient, imbued with a primal energy that hummed beneath his skin. A sense of foreboding settled over him, a prickling awareness that he was not alone.

His eyes, gradually adapting to the gloom, discerned the faint outlines of a vast chamber. Jagged stalactites hung like teeth from the unseen ceiling, and the air was thick with the scent of damp earth and something else... something ancient and faintly familiar.

In the distance, a glow pulsed like a heartbeat. Kyano, drawn by an instinctive curiosity, moved towards it, his footsteps echoing in the cavernous silence. As he drew closer, the glow resolved into a sphere of swirling light, suspended in mid-air as if defying the very laws of gravity.

He recognized it instantly. This was his inner sanctum, a hidden realm within his own consciousness, the place where his very powers taught him how to wield sentient weapons and showed him the trials to win the Scythe. But how had he arrived here? And why was his inner sanctum different than it was before? The orb of his energy that was once a talkative and wise blue and black sphere was now a mix of green with silver and more silent than the sound of his own heart.

A wave of panic washed over him. Had something gone wrong with the portal? Was he trapped in this ethereal realm, cut off from both Serinia and Earth? No… that simply could not happen. He felt his energy when he entered the portal, he was definitely on his way to Serinia.

"Are you going to stand there all day or say something?" asked the orb, jolting Kyano out of his daydream. The voice was different too now. It was not that of an old wise man. This voice was that of a woman. A sarcastic yet assertive voice that somehow had overthrown the old man Kyano grew to like.

"Where am I?" Kyano asked, "And who are you?"

"I clearly overestimated you," the sphere retorted, "A warrior of light indeed… you can't even recognize your own inner sanctum!"

"How can I?" Kyano replied, enraged, "Everything is different here. I don't remember my subconscious being a dark dimly lit dungeon and my energy wasn't green and silver, it was blue! And you were a man not a woman!"

"Well, I suppose that is fair!" replied the orb, "When Hayada changed everything, I changed as well so I suppose an explanation is overdue."

"I would say so," Kyano asserted. He crossed his arms and waited to hear more.

"When Hayada put you back in our old life, you matured and so did I. You lost your memories of me and how to contact me and so you were never able to come here but I am a being of light descended from the serpent of creation himself. I do not forget. And so I waited and waited for the day you would remember something…. Anything. Your powers grew as well unbeknownst to you. I can only surmise that this happened as a direct result of Hayada interfering with your fate. Your powers grew to help compensate and balance that act of hers. I grew, got stronger and evolved," continued the orb.

"It's just funny that you evolved from an old man to a young woman," interrupted Kyano, clearly still irked by the sarcasm he was displayed earlier.

"Hear me out, will you!" scoffed the orb and continued, "When I evolved so did your beast of lore, Marailos, who is now a thunder dragon. A creature of utmost ferocity and power that has God like speed and a few magical tricks that include an ability to change form to other mystical creatures and explosive energy blasts that can wipe out whole mountains."

"That's enough of that," came Marailos's voice and the green and silver orb split into two, one green and one silver. Kyano instantly recognized the silver orb as being Marailos, "Marailos!" he exclaimed, "I never thought I would see you again!"

He reached out towards the sphere, his fingers trembling with a mixture of apprehension and anticipation. As he touched the light, a jolt of energy surged through him, and a torrent of images flooded his mind.

He saw visions of Serinia, ravaged by war and shrouded in darkness. He saw Layana and Merata, their faces etched with worry and exhaustion, their spirits flickering like embers in the face of overwhelming despair. He saw the Scythe, its once vibrant aura now morphed, its power blazing out of control as it attacked everything in its path. He saw Layana in a meditative state, unmoving, her power enveloping the whole city of Laira protecting it from Raka and the Scythe alike. His heart ached for his sister and what she was going through in that moment, but the visions disappeared as quickly as they appeared, "Focus!" interrupted the orb.

"There is much you do not know about Serinia!" Marailos said, "You would do well to hear the green one."

"When you were unceremoniously taken from this world, the Raka that remained retreated into the dark lands. Since there was no human presence there, they festered and evolved themselves, developing the ability to speak, I recall you encountered two such Raka yourself on Earth. Hayada has let them run wild but has also been recruiting them for her own misdeeds both in Serinia and across the mirror. They grew in numbers very quickly without a master to subdue their ferocity and control their rage and began attacking every human settlement and turning Serinia into a wasteland. There are still a few pockets of human settlements spread throughout, but they mostly live underground. The only remaining human city remains to be Laira, protected by a warrior of light, your sister, Layana. She went into an indefinite state of meditation so she could keep using her power to envelop the city with a shield of energy and protect it from harm. The Scythe of Serinia did not return to Dimarius and instead, stayed on to wreak havoc unchecked. With warriors of light unable to tame its power it travels the world and unleashes tornados of pure energy that destroy everything in their path, another reason for human settlements to move underground. Your friend Merata left Laira to pursue the Scythe, as its last wielder to get it to calm down and become silent again but has thus far been unsuccessful. Every time she tries, she is denied by the Scythe, and it continues its outrageous onslaught of brutality endlessly," the green orb concluded.

Kyano heard the story in stunned silence. He could not believe the dangers and the trials that his sister and friend were having to endure, and it brought him unimaginable guilt of not being with them in their desperate time of need. The question, the undeniable, excruciatingly painful question kept gnawing at his mind. Was this what they defeated Daryudan for? Was this the price they had to pay to be rid of the dark lord?

"You will have to steal your resolve and bring hope back to Serinia!" the orb stated.

"What about Hayada?" Kyano replied, "She is about to subdue Earth on the other side! We are mere weeks away from her gaining the ability to read the thoughts of everyone out there. We need to stop her too!"

"Then there is a chance she might overthrow the balance," Marailos said to the orb.

"You are right," replied the green one, "If she can enslave the other side of the mirror, she will have enough power to reshape that world and tip the scales of time, empowering the serpent of Death."

"Hold on!" Kyano interrupted, "Do you know what Hayada is planning to do on Earth?"

"From what you have told us, she is trying to enslave humanity," Marailos replied, "If Hayada can control everyone on Earth, she will be able to tip the scales of balance dictated by time. She will be able to combine life and death, light and darkness and usher a new era of madness, void of free will. If she achieves this on Earth it will have dire consequences for Serinia. What they are I know not!"

"Oh, what the hell!" exclaimed Kyano, "Can things get any worse? This is ridiculous. We have Hayada, who is a god trying to take control of a whole planet and then we have the Scythe running amok and Raka everywhere and only a few weeks to deal with all of it! Where in this obviously hopeless scenario do you see a path that I can take which will resolve all of these time consuming and potentially unwinnable situations?"

Both balls of energy fell silent. Kyano slumped down to the ground, overwhelmed with what he just heard. He put his head in his hands and took a few deep breaths, which felt like a waste of time, his sub consciousness willing him, pushing him to act, to do something to fight someone, to try and make things right, the guilt in his heart plowing away at his own will, weighing him down. He broke down and started to weep. Tears of anger and anguish flooding his very being, his very core shaken and disturbed.

"What should I do?" he asked, his voice a faint wisp between staggered breaths, tears flooding down his face.

"You must acquire the Scyte!" Marailos replied, "You must find the Raka stronghold and wipe it out and you must free Layana and Merata from their quests. Then you can all head to Earth and fight Hayada. Do not give up, young one," he continued, "There is still a chance. With your grown powers, you may be able to tame the Scythe, perhaps even make it a companion on your journey. With the Scythe in your hands again, you will be able to stand up against Hayada and fight on equal footing, regardless of if she enslaves Earth or not. The Scythe has the power to vanquish evil; to bring life back to Serinia, it is the answer to all that troubles you and your kind."

"I couldn't bring forth any of my power on Earth!" Kyano replied, "I can't fight Hayada there."

"You couldn't bring out your power because you didn't know how to connect with your altered powers," replied the green one, "Now that you do, you will be able to freely traverse between Serinia and Earth through here, for this, your inner sanctum, my home, is a bridge between the two worlds that raised you, warrior of light."

The green orb pulsed with a warm, reassuring light. "This is not the end, Kyano," it soothed. "This is a new beginning. You have faced trials before, overcome challenges that seemed insurmountable. You have the strength within you to face this darkness, to restore balance to Serinia and protect the Earth."

Marailos's silver light flared in agreement. "We are with you, Kyano. We will guide you, lend you our strength. You are not alone in this fight."

Kyano, his tears subsiding, felt a spark of resolve ignite within him. He looked at the orbs, his heart swelling with gratitude. "Thank you," he whispered, his voice thick with emotion. "I won't let you down."

He rose to his feet as he took a deep breath and opened his determined eyes. A portal appeared, swirling, inviting, waves of warm air emanating from its edges. He could feel the pull of Serinia, the urgency of his mission. He had to return, to face the chaos, to find Layana and Merata, to tame the Scythe, and to confront Hayada.

With a deep breath, he stepped towards the portal, his heart pounding with a mix of fear and determination. He was ready to face whatever awaited him, to fight for his world, his family, his destiny.

As he disappeared into the swirling energy, the green and silver orbs merged, their combined light illuminating the darkness of the inner sanctum. They waited, their silent vigil a testament to their unwavering faith in the warrior of light.

CHAPTER

12

A History of altered Memories

The funeral ceremony for the prince of Serin was carried out in a glorious manner. In a manner that befitted the feats of bravery and the sacrifice that his death meant to the people of Serinia. The body was paraded through the city streets on its way to the altar of life. The temple of Saan met, the god of passing stood tall and silent as noblemen and citizens alike poured into its courtyard to get one last look at the warrior of light that mysteriously died in the battle that ended the warlord's reign.

Merata was the head of the honor guard for the procession. She held aloft a ceremonial lance wrapped in gold and gemstones; a weapon never used for war but used to welcome departed souls to the afterlife. They passed through the enormous marble stone arch that opened into the courtyard. Normally a very sullen, quiet place where people paid respects to their dearly departed, was now a bustling crowd of onlookers. Some eyes showed a longing and sorrow while some others just looked like they wanted to see the prince. The silence was what was surprising to her. All the people who stood there watching in awe, all the people that stood there out of obligation, there were only a few that seemed genuinely saddened by the event. The joy of victory over evil was too great to sully with sorrow of a warrior's passing it seemed.

Brushing aside the tinge of anger she felt at this display of brazen disrespect, she walked on, solemnly, at a steady pace. There had to be a lot of Lairans and Serinians who were angered by this treachery of fate, she thought. There had to be someone other than the few that knew and loved him that mourned his loss, for what he accomplished during his life was a miracle that even gods couldn't achieve.

She led the procession all the way to the end of the courtyard, to the altar of life. A ceremonial altar, used to cremate kings, queens and others from the royal family. The altar stood pensively surrounded by columns of black marble on either side, each one etched with history and events that shaped Laira's present. Statues of past rulers, looking down at the altar completed what was the most ornate display of eternal respect for a passing soul. Kyano's body was gently placed atop the altar and the priest of the temple took stage to begin the ceremony.

"Today, we gather to bid farewell to perhaps the most decorated warrior we have seen in the history of Serinia," he began, "For he, Kyano Thrinio, fallen prince, brother and friend, fought for us, he dared the very destiny that befell our existence, he stood tall in the face of calamity and paved the way for a new tomorrow, for all of us,"

Layana stood next to the priest, shock and anguish littered her otherwise serene eyes.

"But alas," the priest continued, his voice heavy with sorrow, "Fate is a cruel mistress, and even the bravest of hearts can be extinguished in an instant. Though Kyano's light may have been dimmed, his spirit will forever burn bright in the annals of our history."

He raised his hands towards the heavens, his voice echoing through the courtyard. "Oh, Saan, god of passing, we commend Kyano's soul to your care. Guide him to the realm of eternal peace, where he may find solace and rest after his valiant struggles."

Layana stepped forward, her eyes brimming with tears. She gently placed a wreath of white lilies upon Kyano's chest, a symbol of his purity and sacrifice. Her voice, though choked with emotion, resonated with strength and love.

"My brother, my friend, my hero," she whispered, her words carried on the gentle breeze. "I know you are not gone! I know this is some kind of cruel magic or trick and I vow to you that we will find you and bring you back. Everyone here sees a fallen brother, but I know. I know in my core that you are alive. I know you will come back to us, to me!"

She paused, her gaze sweeping across the assembled crowd. "Kyano may be gone, but his spirit lives on in each of us. Let us honor his memory by carrying his torch, by fighting for the ideals he held dear, by never giving up hope, even in the face of overwhelming darkness."

Her own beliefs aside, she couldn't show her people what she really thought. For if her thoughts were true, she would appear mad to her populace and in the event that her brother was indeed, truly dead, she shuddered to think that perhaps she really was in denial and refused to accept the bitter truth that lay in front of her.

A collective gasp arose from the crowd as a brilliant light emanated from Kyano's body. The white lilies burst into full bloom, their petals glowing with an ethereal luminescence. The air crackled with energy, and a sense of peace and serenity washed over the courtyard.

The priest raised his hands in awe. "Saan has heard our prayers," he declared, his voice filled with wonder. "Kyano's spirit has found its way to the realm of eternal peace."

The priest's words echoed in Layana's ears, but his tone was what caught her attention. He was *surprised* that the flowers burst into an energy flame. As Kyano's body incinerated, she knew for certain that what burned on that altar was a mere effigy. An illusion of flesh and blood that dissipated with fire.

Layana, her tears flowing freely now, smiled through her grief. "Be strong, my brother," she whispered. "May your journey be filled with light and love until we meet again."

The crowd, moved by the spectacle and Layana's heartfelt words, erupted in a chorus of farewells and blessings. The sound echoed through the courtyard, a testament to the profound impact Kyano had had on their lives.

As the light faded and Kyano's body was consumed by the flames of the altar, a single white feather drifted down from the sky, landing gently on Layana's outstretched palm. She clutched it to her heart, a tangible reminder of her brother's enduring spirit.

Though Kyano was gone, his legacy would live on, inspiring generations to come with his courage, his compassion, and his unwavering belief in the power of good.

The peace that followed Daryudan's defeat was a balm to Serinia's wounds. The scars of war remained, etched deep into the land and its people, but a fragile hope bloomed amidst the ruins. Laira, once a bastion of resistance, became a beacon of renewal, its walls expanding to accommodate the influx of refugees and settlers seeking a new beginning.

Farmers returned to their fields, their plows turning the fertile soil, coaxing life from the scarred earth. Merchants reopened their stalls, their wares a vibrant tapestry of colors and textures. Children's laughter echoed through the streets; a melody of innocence that had been muted for far too long.

But in the shadowed depths of the dark lands, a different kind of resurgence was taking place. The Raka, those monstrous creatures born of darkness and rage, had not been vanquished with Daryudan's fall. They lurked in the shadows, their numbers swelling, their hatred festering. They were leaderless, their primal instincts driving them towards a singular, destructive purpose: the annihilation of humankind.

Two years of uneasy peace shattered with the sudden ferocity of a thunderclap. Whispers of Raka attacks on outlying settlements reached Laira, tales of brutal massacres and villages reduced to smoldering ruins.

Fear, a chilling specter, crept back into the hearts of the Serinians, casting a pall over their hard-won peace.

Then, the unthinkable happened. A vast Raka horde, ten thousand strong, emerged from the dark lands, their monstrous forms a terrifying tide of darkness sweeping towards Laira. The city's defenses, still weakened from the war, were ill-prepared for such an onslaught. Panic gripped the city, the joyous celebrations of the past two years replaced by the chilling dread of impending doom.

Layana and Merata led what was left of the human forces against the attacking monsters. A hard felt battle ensued. Laira being unprepared meant that Layana had to hold back her powers. She couldn't destroy everything in her path only to kill the Raka and destroy the fields and villages surrounding Laira. It had to be a surgical approach which meant the battle would drag on and it would take longer to subdue the invading Raka horde.

Veraqua, the ancient one, the enormous dragon that aided Merata during the great war departed as soon as Daryudan was defeated. Having fulfilled the pact he made with Merata in that desolate mountain cave, having helped the human armies defeat the dark lord, he disappeared, never to be heard from again. He wouldn't answer Merata's call and both Layana and she found themselves weakened by his absence.

Yet, they battled on, holding the Lairan stronghold against wave after wave of Raka attacks, that lasted 8 months to fight the Raka while protecting Laira's assets. The human army lost a third of its soldiers. The Raka having no leader meant the only way to defeat them was to kill them all. Like a farmer battling locusts with nothing but insecticide to spray on them, knowing the locusts will not stop until they all died, Layana and Merata fought on, leading their army step by step, holding the front lines and advancing on what seemed like a relentless horde of evil locusts.

The sky grew dark with no warning that day. A tempest of lightning and raw power engulfed their tired army as the wrath of the Scythe descended upon the battle. A whirlwind of its power swept across the Raka, cleansing the land of any that were unlucky enough to be in its path.

Merata and Layana looked on in horror, helpless, shocked at the sight of the Scythe of Serinia ripping their enemies and their allies to shreds as it cleansed the land of evil once again. With the Raka army vanquished the Scythe disappeared as quickly and suddenly as it appeared.

The aftermath of the battle was a scene of devastation. The once fertile fields surrounding Laira were now scarred and blackened, littered with the mangled remains of Raka and humans alike. The air hung heavy with the stench of death and burnt flesh.

Layana and Merata stood amidst the carnage, their bodies weary, their spirits heavy with grief. The victory felt hollow, the cost too high. They had repelled the Raka horde, but at a terrible price.

Layana surveyed the destruction, her heart aching for the fallen. "What have we done?" she whispered, her voice barely audible above the mournful cries of the wounded, "We took too long and the Scythe..." she trailed off.

Merata placed a comforting hand on her shoulder. "We did what we had to do," she said, her voice firm. "We protected Laira. We honored Kyano's memory."

Layana nodded, a tear tracing a path down her cheek. "But at what cost?" she murmured, her gaze falling upon the fallen soldiers, their faces frozen in eternal agony.

The Scythe's intervention had been both a blessing and a curse. It had saved them from certain defeat, but it had also unleashed its indiscriminate wrath upon friend and foe alike. The power of the weapon, once a symbol of hope, now felt like a terrifying force beyond their control.

"We need to find it," Merata declared, her eyes filled with a steely determination. "We need to understand why it's behaving this way."

Layana looked at her, a flicker of hope igniting in her eyes. "You think we can control it?"

Merata nodded. "We have to. The fate of Serinia depends on it."

For weeks after that battle ended, reports came more frequently of a tornado of pure energy destroying fields and settlements ruthlessly. The attacks were random and there was no pattern, no rhyme or reason for why this was happening and where the Scythe would strike next.

Merata buried herself in research. Searching for clues and reasons for the scythe's behavior when one day, she found a hint.

"My lady," said Adrom, a frail elderly scholar, "The Scythe seems to be attacking any area that still has remnants of Raka energy."

Adrom was undoubtedly one of the most respected scholars in all of Laira. He enjoyed teaching his trade and training new librarians to take over for him when he would eventually retire. Although his age prevented his body from being more efficient, it could never dampen the sharpness of his mind.

"It attacked here, at Laira, the first ground fall of its energy happened at the very site Daryudan was slain," he said, confident in his theory.

"Please explain more," Merata asked. There was no time for her to dwell on how Adrom arrived at this conclusion. She could not spare time for pleasantries either. She needed to know what was going on.

"Its next attack was at the ancient grounds of the Rycana, the same place where his highness, prince Kyano, fought with Tenemasa," Adrom continued, "I have checked the location of all ten attacks that have happened thus far and they are all consistent with this. The Scythe is following a trail of Raka energy from the strongest to the weakest is what I can summarize."

"How confident are you with this?" Layana asked, "Can you predict where it will strike next?"

"I can make a few assumptions but without accurate data of how much Raka energy is left in which location, I cannot say for certain," he replied, "There is still Raka energy left here in Laira as well so we may see it attack us yet again my lady," he added solemnly.

"The Scythe may be powerful but without a wielder to focus its rage, the amount of power it unleashes is not unsurmountable," Layana said, "But it is still the Scythe of Serinia, and I can't hold it off without some drastic measures," a hit of hesitation and fear crept in to her tone as she finished.

"And I think I know where to look for it," Merata added, "I have a few places in mind. Every battle that happened between Kyano coming to Serinia and now is a possible strike location and if we leave immediately, we can visit these places and try to get the Scythe back!"

"I can't leave Laira," Layana said, "It's too risky. We don't know if more Raka will attack, and we don't know if the Scythe will attack again. I must stay here and protect my kingdom. But you Merata," she said, a definite sound of plea in her voice, "You must find it, you must stop it! I will keep our people safe no matter the cost while you venture out and find the Scythe. I am proud to call myself your friend, your sister and there is no one else alive that I would trust with this mission." A tear rolled down her face and Merata could tell, those memories of Kyano still haunted Layana, "Who knows," Layana continued, "Maybe you will even find him and bring him back again!"

Merata gripped Layans' hands as she said those words, "I will do everything I can and die trying if I have to, but I will not return to Laira until I stop the Scythe your highness."

Layana decided to go into a meditative state to form a shield of her own energy around Laira. For all the destruction wrought by the Scythe, Layana could tell that when it came, the energy released by the Scythe was something that she could protect against. The scythe was not at full power without a wielder and Layana saw an opportunity to protect her citizens from its indiscriminate attacks. But there was a cost, she couldn't keep an endless loop of her energy coursing through her being and the shield without being incapacitated. She had to be still. She had to be for the lack of a better term, unconscious and unaware of her immediate surroundings to focus all that she had on maintaining the barrier.

Merata watched Layana settle into her meditative trance, a shimmering dome of protective energy slowly enveloping the city of Laira. A bittersweet ache settled in her heart. Layana, their fearless leader, their beacon of hope, was now a prisoner of her own power, sacrificing her freedom for the safety of her people. She handpicked a group of soldiers, Saldah being their captain, to guard the Queen of Laira indefinitely. To guard Layana until she no longer needed to be in that state anymore.

The reports of the Scythe's rampages had become a terrifying rhythm in their lives – a sudden darkening of the sky, a deafening roar, and then the devastating whirlwind of energy that left nothing but scorched earth and shattered lives in its wake. The Scythe, once a symbol of hope and liberation, was now a rogue force, its power unleashed and uncontrolled, a terrifying echo of the war they had so desperately fought to win.

Merata knew she couldn't stand idly by while her world crumbled around her. Layana had entrusted her with a mission: to find the Scythe, to understand its erratic behavior, and to bring it back under control. It was a daunting task, one that filled her with trepidation, but she wouldn't shirk her responsibility. She owed it to Layana, to Kyano, to all of Serinia.

With a heavy heart but a resolute spirit, Merata prepared to embark on her quest. She gathered her weapons, donned her armor, and mounted her loyal steed. As she rode out of the gates of Laira, the shimmering dome of Layana's protective energy a constant reminder of the stakes, she cast one last glance back at the city.

"I won't fail you, Layana," she whispered, her voice carried on the wind. "I will find the Scythe. I will bring it back." And with that promise echoing in her ears, she turned her gaze towards the horizon, towards the unknown dangers that awaited her, towards the heart of the storm.

CHAPTER

13

A Failed Reveal

The Mirage office was unusually quiet. The usual clatter of keyboards and the murmur of reporters' discussions were replaced by a somber stillness. Miranda and Jeremiah sat across from Mr. Vargus, their faces etched with grief and determination. After a lot of careful consideration and even more hide and seek with the plethora of CCTV cameras spread around the city, Miranda and Jeremiah made it to the office of the Mirage.

The one advantage they had in this entire ordeal being that V5 was unaware of Jeremiah being involved now. Once Kyano went through the portal at the university, Miranda made herself scarce. She escaped as quickly as she could, making sure to cover her tracks. She left her car at the university and took a bus to go back to Jeremiah's house.

With the cunning that he possessed, Jeremiah made sure to keep Miranda hidden. V5 and the police had been to his house inquiring about *Josh* and if he had come home recently. They had even searched his home top to bottom but found nothing. *Josh* was nowhere to be found. Making sure not to be followed, Jeremiah went to the apartment, to 1653 Blairwood Cove where he was keeping Miranda hidden.

That morning, they left the apartment early, making sure to keep out of sight of any and all cameras. With the reach and influence that V5 had, there was no telling who was their spy, willingly or not. Miranda snuck into the back of Jeremiah's car, and he drove carefully to the Mirage's office. With a baseball cap and a dust mask on, pretending to be sick, Miranda followed him inside as they made their way to the 11th floor on foot.

The receptionist was happy to see Jeremiah. Only having seen him at the occasional Christmas party to which the family was invited, it was a pleasure for Gary to see Jeremiah again. Hoping that there was some news about Josh, Gary ushered the Mirage's unannounced guests into Mr. Vargus's office.

"I assume you are here to tell me where two of my rookies have disappeared to," Mr. Vargus said as soon as he saw them, "I never thought Josh would go dark like this, it's not like him. I expected this from Adam but no, not Josh."

"Mr. Vargus," Miranda began, her voice trembling slightly, "we have some news."

Mr. Vargus looked at them, his brow furrowed with skepticism. "What is it? Do Josh and Adam want to quit and just don't have the guts to tell me that?" He was not holding his irritation back at all.

"Adam... Adam is dead," Jeremiah said, his voice heavy with sorrow. "V5 killed him."

Mr. Vargus's eyes widened in shock. "Killed him? How?"

Miranda took a deep breath, steeling herself for the difficult task of recounting the events of the past few days. She described what she was doing at V5, how she found inconsistencies in the code and what had happened when she went to the research floor.

Mr. Vargus listened in stunned silence, his face pale with disbelief. "I... I can't believe it," he stammered. "Adam... he was a goof ball for sure but this! This is illegal and inhuman!"

He looked at them, his expression hardening with resolve. "What about Josh?" he asked. "Is he...?"

Miranda shook her head. "After what I found in that torture chamber, I was the one who called and left the voicemail with your office. Adam and Josh were on the trail of the breadcrumbs that I left but it was only going to be a matter of time before V5 discovered me and they did. They took me to the same torture chamber and were going to kill me when Adam and Josh rescued me."

Mr. Vargus sighed, his shoulders slumping with the weight of the news. "I was afraid you were going to say that. They should have called the cops, those idiots!"

"They didn't have time Mr. Vargus," Miranda replied, "Quite frankly, I would not be alive if they waited for the police," continuing her tale, she narrated what happened next, "Adam, Josh and I were running down the stairwell when we got caught again. In that scuffle, Adam was... Adam was killed. Josh stayed behind to fight them off and I ran for my life. I don't know where Josh is right now, but it looked like he was escaping too when we fled. As I left the stairwell, I saw him running down behind me. I just assumed he ran in a different direction than me after I left the building."

He looked at them, his eyes filled with a mix of grief and determination. "We need to expose V5," he said, his voice firm. "We need to tell the world what they're doing."

Miranda nodded. "We agree. That's why we're here."

She reached into her bag and pulled out the thumb drive containing the evidence she had collected. "We have proof," she said, handing the drive to Mr. Vargus. "Photos, videos, everything."

Mr. Vargus took the drive, his fingers closing around it tightly. "This is huge," he said, his voice filled with a mix of awe and apprehension. "But are you sure it's enough? V5 is powerful. They could easily discredit you, claim this is all a fabrication."

Jeremiah spoke up, his voice firm. "We're willing to testify, Mr. Vargus. We'll tell the world what we saw, what we know."

Miranda nodded in agreement. "We won't let them get away with this."

Mr. Vargus looked at them, his eyes filled with admiration. "I knew I could count on you," he said. "The Mirage will publish this story. We'll expose V5 for what they are."

He stood up, his voice ringing with conviction. "We'll do it for Adam."

The portal shimmered, a tear in the fabric of reality, bridging the fiery depths of the Netherworld with the sterile confines of Hayada's office. Daryudan stepped through, his senses assaulted by the sudden shift from the oppressive heat and sulfurous stench of his prison to the cool, air-conditioned atmosphere and the faint scent of lavender and expensive perfume.

Hayada gestured towards a plush armchair. "Welcome to my world, Daryudan," she said, a sly smile playing on her lips. "Or rather, a world ripe for the taking."

Daryudan surveyed the room, his eyes lingering on the panoramic window overlooking the sprawling cityscape. "It is... different," he remarked, his voice a low rumble.

"Indeed," Hayada agreed. "But no less corrupt, no less deserving of our intervention."

She turned towards a nearby table, where a neatly folded pile of clothes lay waiting. "First things first," she said, handing him the garments. "A change of attire is in order. We wouldn't want to attract undue attention."

Daryudan examined the clothes – a tailored suit, crisp white shirt, and a silk tie. He raised an eyebrow. "This is...unfamiliar."

"Consider it a necessary adaptation," Hayada replied. "We must blend in before we can disrupt."

She snapped her fingers, and two hulking figures emerged from the shadows. Their faces were obscured by dark masks, but their eyes glowed with an eerie, reptilian intensity. Daryudan recognized the predatory aura that emanated from them. Raka.

"These are your escorts," Hayada explained. "They will appraise of what we are doing here and teach you how to blend in. You will need to learn a few things and understand how this world operates which I am sure the Raka can easily show you through their minds. They will then assist you in your first task."

Daryudan's interest piqued. "And what task is that?"

"A simple kidnapping," Hayada said, her voice devoid of emotion. "Miranda Hawthorne. She has proven to be a thorn in my side. But she possesses knowledge. The knowledge to accelerate my plan and remove any weaknesses from this mortal wonder of technology."

One of the Raka stepped forward, his voice a guttural rasp. "We have been monitoring the city's surveillance feeds. It appears the woman Hawthorne and an older male accomplice recently visited the Mirage newspaper office."

Hayada's eyes narrowed. "The Mirage? Interesting. It seems our meddling project manager has a penchant for attracting troublesome allies."

She turned towards Daryudan, her voice laced with chilling authority. "Find them, Daryudan. Eliminate the reporters at the Mirage and bring Miranda to me. She will complete programming Kira and fulfil the job that I granted her."

Daryudan's lips curled into a predatory smile. "Consider it done."

The clatter of the keyboard filled the otherwise silent office, punctuated by the occasional murmurs of Miranda and Jeremiah as they clarified details and verified facts. Mr. Vargus, his brow furrowed in concentration, typed with a furious intensity, his fingers flying across the keys. The article was taking shape, a damning exposé of V5's sinister secrets, a testament to Adam's sacrifice and Josh's disappearance.

Hours blurred into a late-night marathon fueled by coffee and adrenaline. The clock ticked past midnight, the only sound in the deserted building the rhythmic tapping of keys and the rustle of paper. As Mr. Vargus put the finishing touches on the piece, a sudden *ding* echoed through the office, signaling the front door opening.

Confusion rippled through the room. Who else would be visiting the Mirage at this hour?

The sliding front doors slid open, and a figure emerged, his imposing frame filling the doorway. Daryudan. His eyes, burning with a malevolent intensity, scanned the room, settling on the three figures huddled around the computer. Two Raka assassins flanked him, their faces obscured by dark masks, their hands twitching towards the weapons concealed beneath their cloaks.

"Daryudan!" Jeremiah gasped, a look of shock and denial spread across his face. This was not expected but he knew there was no leaving that building alive. All he could do, if there was anything, was he could make an attempt to give Miranda and Mr. Vargus a chance to escape.

Jeremiah reacted instantly. With a swift motion, he manifested an energy sword, its blade humming with a vibrant blue light. He lunged forward, intercepting the Raka assassins before they could reach Mr. Vargus. The office erupted in a flurry of motion and blinding flashes of as Jeremiah's sword clashed against the Raka's dark weapons.

Despite his age, Jeremiah moved with surprising agility and ferocity, his swordsmanship honed through years of training in Serinia. He parried and thrust, his blade a whirlwind of blue energy, forcing the Raka assassins back. One by one, they fell, their bodies dissolving into shadows, leaving behind only the lingering echo of their dying screams.

But as Jeremiah turned to face Daryudan, a crushing blow sent him reeling. He crumpled to the floor, unconscious, his sword clattering away from his grasp and dissipating into nothing.

Daryudan advanced towards Mr. Vargus, his eyes filled with a cold, predatory gleam. Mr. Vargus, unarmed and defenseless, could only stare in horror as the warlord raised his hand, a dark energy coalescing around his fist. The air crackled with power, and a surge of dark energy erupted from Daryudan's hand, striking Mr. Vargus with the force of a thunderbolt.

The editor slumped in his chair, his eyes wide with shock, his life extinguished in an instant.

Daryudan turned his attention to Miranda, his lips curling into a cruel smile. "You and I have much to discuss," he said, his voice a low, menacing growl, "Help your friend get up. I am not going to kill you both," he said.

Dazed and shocked, Miranda did as she was told. She struggled to lift Jeremiah off the floor and onto a nearby couch, still shaking, unsure if this was to be her last night alive. She tried to calm herself as best she could and turned to face Daryudan, awaiting what was to come next.

"The Raka are mindlessly loyal to me," Daryudan began, sending a tremor of uncertainty through Miranda. This was not the conversation she was expecting. "You see, I am the one who created them and no matter how many iterations of these beasts emerge, I am their one true master and as such, they cannot keep secrets from me," a smile rippled across his lips as he struggled to keep the entirety of his plan to himself.

He was going to do the unthinkable. "Tell me," He continued, "What became of the warrior who saved you?"

"You mean Josh?" Miranda asked, still defiant, hiding Kyano's true name.

"I mean Kyano," Daryudan responded, the assertiveness in his voice clearly conveying to her not to hide anything in her words, "Where did he go?"

Judging by what Miranda knew of Daryudan from Kyano's words, this was no mere person. This was not someone to trifle with and yet here he was, a warlord who ravaged an entire civilization for six millennia, sitting across from her, having a conversation. She thought it best to hear him out without irritating him and the only way to do that was to tell him the truth.

"I don't know," she replied, "I think he went to Serinia. We went to the university and opened a portal using a plasma generator."

"So, he is across the mirror now," Daryudan considered.

"I suppose," Miranda replied, "I didn't see where he went, just that the portal opened, and he disappeared is what I know."

"Very well," Daryudan said, "What do you know about this earpiece?"

"I know it gives Hayada the ability to hear everyone's thoughts," replied Miranda, "Although I imagine the A.I., Kira would be the one listening and not Hayada herself. She would have to access Kira through a computer or interface of some kind to know everything."

"That is where you come in," Daryudan interrupted, "I will give you one chance mortal, one chance to save your life. You possess the knowledge of this A.I you speak of, and you possess enough cunning to open a portal without magic. You will create a means for Hayada's consciousness to merge with Kira."

Miranda considered what she just heard. Considered those words very carefully. She was not sure if Daryudan intended to say what he did but in saying those words, he gave Miranda an idea. A very big idea. One that could change the course of everything and end this battle.

"I know V5 has neural links on the research floor," she continued, "It's used as a way to interact with Kira and speed up the processing instead of typing endless commands which takes longer. If we can rewire one of these neural links to a concept drive, Kira could download herself into the mind of the user. Afterall, the code to do this is already there. This process is already in Kira, this process is how Kira will be able to hear the thoughts of all of the users of Vbuddy. But she can't invade their minds because the earpiece is not powerful enough to bridge this transaction. The neural links at V5 should be able to, however, in theory." Miranda felt she might have said more than she needed to, but the words just came out of her. The fear of what she was faced with too great to swallow, she used the only weapon she had, her brain, to blurt out the solution that the dark lord was looking for. However, if there was anything that she could gleam from this revelation that she just had, it was the secret. It was the idea she had earlier taking form in her mind and now she knew what had to be done which, hidden in words yet again, would be the last thing she told Daryudan, "If you can take me back to V5, I can program the neural link to do this. Since Kira has access to Vbuddy data, once the earpiece goes live, Hayada will be able to hear everything as it happens."

Daryudan stood up from the chair and walked towards the door, "Follow me, mortal." he said as he walked out of the Mr. Vargus's office, Miranda in tow. As they left the door, two more Raka guards went inside to clean up. With practiced precision, they wrapped up Mr. Vargus's body and cleaned his office, making sure to purge his hard drive and any evidence of the article he had written. "Bring the other mortal with you," Daryudan commanded, "He is our prisoner."

Jeremiah came to as the cleanup Raka did their work. Realizing that they had not noticed him yet, he quietly surveyed his surroundings. He could not see Daryudan or Miranda anywhere and his mind went to the only possible explanation. They must have killed her or kidnapped her. He quietly rose to his feet and formed his sword again. Before the Raka noticed, he snuck up behind the closest one and slit its throat. It slumped to the ground, making gurgling noises as its blood rushed out of its neck; the other monster spun around, just in time to see Jeremiah's sword held high as he lunged into the air. The Raka moved swiftly to the side avoiding Jeremiah's thrust and knocked him at the nape of his neck, rendering him unconscious once more.

Daryudan took Miranda back to V5. Back to the place where it all began where dread and death awaited around every corner. This was the last place Miranda wanted to visit again but in her current situation, it was the only place where she would be alive. Even if it meant only for a little while longer.

The elevator doors slid open with a hushed whisper, revealing the research floor and all its secrets once more. Miranda followed Daryudan quietly as he led her to the neural network lab, knowing all along that she had no choice but to. He motioned for her to sit at the control desk, and she got to work as instructed.

Daryudan left Miranda alone and made his way to Hayada's office. As the doors opened, he could see that she was fuming. She knew that Miranda was in the building. Motioning to the security camera footage from the elevator, Hayada questioned, "Your task was to bring me this mortal Daryudan," she fumed, "Give me one good reason why she is not in front of me right now."

Daryudan, his imposing figure radiating a smug satisfaction, addressed Hayada with a flourish. "I have brought you a gift, my goddess," he announced, his voice resonating with a dark amusement. "A solution to your... limitations."

"The means to transcend your physical form," Daryudan explained, his voice laced with conspiratorial excitement. "To merge your consciousness with Kira, to become omnipresent, omniscient."

Hayada's eyes widened, a flicker of avarice igniting in their depths. The power to be everywhere at once, to know everything, to control every aspect of existence – it was a tantalizing prospect, a dream she had long harbored in the darkest corners of her heart. She knew Kira would have access to all the Vbuddy data and that she would have had to use her computer or a neural interface to access this knowledge, but that plan had a flaw. A limitation. Any damage to the interface, any corruption to its software could result in a temporary loss of her link to Kira but this way, if her consciousness were to merge with Kira, there would be no need for an interface. There would be nothing the mortals could damage to handicap the limitless power she was about to receive. She would not have to rely on Kira to feed her filtered information. She could hear and know everything and decide which information to act on and which to leave alone. She would know immediately which of the users she would brainwash to do her bidding, all the world leaders who would receive the Vbuddy as a gift. Once she invaded their minds, she would control the entire world and its armies and resources.

"And how is this to be achieved?" she inquired, her voice barely concealing her eagerness.

Daryudan straightened himself, a cruel smile twisting his lips. "This woman, Hawthorne, possesses the knowledge to rewire the neural link, to create a conduit for Kira to flow into your consciousness. Kira will live in your mind and give you the power you seek."

Hayada's gaze settled on Daryudan's, her eyes piercing, searching for any hint of deceit or defiance. All she could see was her servant's determination to enable her plan. Not sensing any malice from him, she agreed.

"Very well," Hayada declared, her voice ringing with an imperious authority. "Let it be done."

CHAPTER

14

In the Shadows of Serin

Jimmara lazed about on the grass. Picking fruit for his colony was his least favorite chore to do and he would rather spend his days playing with the other children than foraging in the Sinesian forest. The forest stood still and calm a mere few hundred yards from the desolated kingdom of Serin. Once a beacon of hope and all that was good, Serin, now no more than a destroyed fortress, was a silent reminder that good never always won over evil. Jimmara sat up, bored and defeated and resolved to finish his chore so he could get back to the more important things of his life and play with his friends.

He walked up the riverbank and back into the trees of the forest and looked about for lingua trees. Short and sturdy trees they were, their wood made for long-lasting furniture, but Jimmara was not interested in that at all. He was foraging for the lingua fruit. About the size of two fists, the lingua fruit was a complete meal in its own right. It was enough to fill a stomach and keep one satisfied and the trees that had fruit on them usually had at least ten that could be picked.

After walking around the forest for all of ten minutes, but surely it felt like an eternity to Jimmara, he laid eyes on a lingua tree that had over two dozen ripe fruits. Its branches bending under their weight, ready to be picked. Excited and relieved at his discovery, he hurried over and filled his basket. Carefully examining his loot as he picked them off the tree, he threw away only three fruit that were either too ripe or had holes in them to say insects were inside them and as such were no good for consumption.

As he picked his last fruit, he heard a noise behind him. A twig breaking. As if someone had stepped on it. He turned around suddenly and to his horror, he was face to face with a Raka.

The boy's heart hammered in his chest, a frantic drumbeat against the sudden silence of the forest. He scrambled backwards, his eyes wide with terror, his breath catching in ragged gasps. The Raka, its monstrous form a grotesque silhouette against the dappled sunlight, advanced with a predatory grace that belied its hulking size. Its snarling jaws revealed rows of jagged teeth, and its eyes, burning with a malevolent fire, seemed to pierce through the boy's very soul.

He knew he couldn't outrun the creature. Raka were renowned for their speed and agility, their senses honed for the hunt. But he had to try. He had to reach the safety of the tunnels, the hidden refuge that sheltered his family and friends.

He turned and fled, his small legs pumping furiously, his bare feet pounding against the forest floor. Branches whipped at his face, thorns tore at his clothes, but he didn't dare slow down. The snarling growls of the Raka echoed behind him, a terrifying reminder of the gruesome fate that awaited him if he faltered.

He scrambled over fallen logs, his lungs burning, his legs aching. A dark, moss-covered cove in the base of an ancient oak, loomed ahead, a beacon of hope in the face of despair.

With a final burst of adrenaline, he lunged towards the opening, his fingers grasping at the rough bark. He tumbled through the narrow passage, the darkness swallowing him whole. He hid there in the darkness, praying, hoping that he would not be discovered, as he heard the Raka's frustrated screams emanating from outside his dark refuge. He could hear the footsteps, the unmistakable *thump...thump...* as the Raka drew close and its low guttural gnarls as it searched the area for him.

A deafening silence fell upon him as he waited for the beast and every moment he waited felt like a day. A minute later he peered out from the moss cover to see, and the Raka's hand grabbed his neck from behind, lifting him up into the air like he was a baby bird.

The boy gasped, his vision blurring as the world tilted on its axis. He clawed at the thick, leathery hand encircling his throat, his nails leaving futile scratches on its rough surface. His legs kicked frantically, searching for purchase, but only met with empty air. The Raka's grip tightened, cutting off his air supply, his lungs burning with the desperate need to breathe.

He twisted his head, catching a glimpse of the creature's face. Its eyes, burning with a malevolent glee, seemed to savor his terror. Its snarling jaws were inches from his own, the stench of rotting flesh filling his nostrils.

The boy's struggles weakened, his vision darkening at the edges. He could feel his consciousness slipping away, the darkness closing in like a suffocating blanket. Just as he thought he would lose consciousness, a blinding flash of light erupted, followed by a deafening roar. The Raka's grip loosened, and the boy crumpled to the ground, gasping for air.

He looked up, his vision swimming, and saw a figure standing amidst the swirling dust and dissipating light. A warrior, clad in a silver and green battlesuit, his face obscured by a helmet, stood with a double-edged sword raised, its blade dripping with an eerie green luminescence. The Raka lay motionless at his feet, its body contorted in an unnatural position, its eyes wide with shock and disbelief.

The warrior turned towards the boy, his voice a low pitched hum that echoed through the forest. "Are you alright?"

The boy, still gasping for breath, could only nod, his eyes wide with awe and gratitude. He had been saved.

Kyano knelt beside the trembling boy, his armored hand gently resting on the child's shoulder. "Easy now," he soothed, his voice a rumble beneath the helmet. "You're safe." He reached into a pouch on his belt and produced a water bottle, offering it to the boy. "Here, drink."

The boy, his eyes wide with a mix of fear and awe, shakily took the bottle and drank deeply, the cool water calming his racing heart. He looked up at Kyano, his gaze tracing the intricate details of the warrior's armor, the faint glow of the Fury's scabbard at his side.

"Who... who are you?" the boy stammered, his voice barely a whisper.

Kyano's hand gently removed his helmet, revealing a face etched with concern and determination. "My name is Kyano," he said, his voice warm and reassuring. "And I'm here to help."

The boy's eyes widened further. "Kyano?" he echoed. "But... you're..."

"A ghost?" Kyano finished, a wry smile playing on his lips. "Yes, I suppose I am. But right now, we have more pressing matters to attend to."

He glanced towards the forest's edge, his senses alert. "There are more of those creatures nearby," he said, his voice hardening. "At least ten, maybe more. They're drawn to the scent of fear."

As if to punctuate his words, a chorus of snarls and growls erupted from the depths of the forest, followed by the thunderous pounding of heavy footsteps. The ground vibrated beneath them, and the air crackled with a malevolent energy.

Kyano's eyes narrowed. "Stay here," he commanded, his voice firm. "And don't make a sound."

He rose to his feet, his hand moving to the Fury's hilt. But then, he paused, a different weapon calling to him. He needed something with greater range, something that could strike multiple targets with swift precision.

"Seruga!" he bellowed, his voice echoing through the forest.

A dark shape materialized in his outstretched hand, its form shifting and solidifying into a magnificent bow, its surface shimmering with an obsidian sheen. Seruga, the Bow of Redemption, a weapon forged by the heart of a dragon, its arrows imbued with the very essence of light and vengeance.

Kyano knocked an arrow, his movements fluid and practiced. He drew the string, the energy of the bow humming in harmony with his own. He could sense the Raka approaching, their bloodlust, a palpable wave of darkness crashing towards them.

With a final breath, he released the arrow. It streaked through the air, a beacon of light piercing the gloom of the forest. It struck the lead Raka with pinpoint accuracy, piercing its thick hide and exploding in a burst of radiant energy.

Kyano didn't hesitate. He drew and released, his movements a blur, his arrows finding their marks with deadly precision. The forest echoed with the sounds of snarls turning into shrieks of pain, the thud of heavy bodies collapsing to the ground.

In a matter of seconds, the Raka horde was vanquished, their bodies dissolving into shadows, leaving behind only the echoes of their demise.

Kyano lowered the bow, his breath coming in steady exhales. He turned towards the boy, who stared at him with wide, awestruck eyes.

"Find your way home little one," he told the boy, "There is a tempest on its way." The skies started to darken, lightning dancing across the nimbus in a frenzied manner followed by the unmistakable beat of thunder. The symphony of the Scythe was about to begin. Jimmara scrambled to his feet and ran as fast he could, darting into the woods till he reached the trap door by a boulder shaped like a cat. He pulled it open as quickly as he could and ducked inside but he couldn't will himself to leave.. not yet... not while he could see the returned prince of Serin fight the Scythe of Serinia.

Kyano put his hands together and his bow disappeared. "It's time to break the tempest," he whispered to himself, "Curved Assault!" he screamed, and the familiar black portal opened up behind him. The raging, awe inspiring weapon that he used to cleanse entire battle fields of Raka came forth in all of its crescent splendor. He took a hold of its hilt, and the pressure of its energy sent heat waves emanating away from him with a force big enough to break branches on the trees beside him.

With swift and precise movements, he swung his blade around, its energy whirring, its frequency growing in pitch with every movement. All the while, his watchful eyes looked at the tornado unfolding overhead, waiting for his chance to intercept its attack.

"Dawn of Mayhem!" he cried as he swung his blade upward toward the sky, toward the Scythe and the Curved Assault released is pent up energy. It came forth with a force Kyano had never felt from the weapon before. It was as though the weapon itself was waiting, eagerly waiting to be released and now that it had found its opportunity, it was going to fight with all it had. The energy wave from Kyano's attack hit the Scythe's tornado head on and they clashed in a spectacle of blinding light and unmoving will.

As Kyano's wave weakened, so did the Scythe's assault and the tornado moved back to regroup. It swung around like a pendulum and started at Kyano with blinding speed and Kyano released another wave from his crescent weapon, "Dawn of Mayhem!" He screamed again and the wave came forth, bigger and stronger than before and the dance continued.

The exchanges went back and forth a few times until the clouds above started to lighten, Kyano could sense the Scythe was about to leave.

Thinking quickly, he said, "Marailos!" and his thunder dragon appeared. Kyano jumped onto its back as soon as it manifested, not bothering with any pleasantries, he just said, "Follow that Scythe!" and in the blink of an eye and flash of silver light, the dragon disappeared and was next seen in the sky next to the Scythe. Kyano battled with it yet again, exchanging blows as if in a sword fight, parrying its attacks and thrusting into its handle away from its blade.

Just as he had predicted, a portal began to open behind the Scythe and with the speed of his thunder dragon, Kyano followed it into the portal and they both disappeared to reveal a blue spotless sky. The forest below came alive again with a cool breeze, force of the wind dissipating after the tornado. Jimmara watched the entire exchange from his grounded perch. "No one is going to believe this!" he said to himself.

The swirling vortex of the portal spat Kyano out onto solid ground with an unceremonious thud. He gasped, his senses reeling from the abrupt transition. The oppressive darkness of the portal gave way to a blinding luminescence, and the scentless void was replaced by the crisp, invigorating air of a mountaintop. The Curved Assault and Marailos had both dematerialized in transit and Kyano quickly checked with his inner energy to make sure they were both safe and back in his being.

The mountain top was as advertised, open to the skies above with a sea of clouds below it, lightning and thunder rippling across them portraying a brewing storm and impending rain to the lands below. The air was crisp and cold, snow flew and danced freely in the wind as the sun beat down from above, its heat barely a solace against the chill of the mountain.

He staggered to his feet, his eyes struggling to adjust to the sudden brilliance. As Kyano gathered his bearings he began to realize that the mountain top could not be that bright from the slanted winter sun gleaming down on it. The light was coming from elsewhere. It was coming from a being standing in front of him. An imposing figure, that exuded power and authority. There was a feeling of kindness in the air, a drastic paradox given the place he was at. Golden light streamed from this creature and Kyano's eyes took longer than he expected to be able to see who it was that was standing in front of him.

Dimarius. The King of Gods.

CHAPTER

15

Back to Where it Began

The air hung heavy with the scent of damp earth and decaying leaves as Merata navigated the labyrinthine tunnels of the Sinesian settlement. Torches flickered, casting dancing shadows on the rough-hewn walls, illuminating the worried faces of the inhabitants who lined her path. Whispers followed her like shadows, their voices hushed with a mix of fear and reverence.

She reached the central chamber, where the settlement's elder, a wizened woman with eyes that held the wisdom of generations, awaited her. Merata bowed her head in respect.

"Elder Elara," she greeted, her voice carrying through the hushed chamber. "I seek your wisdom."

Elara gestured towards a rough-hewn bench. "Sit, Merata, warrior of light. Tell me what brings you to our humble abode."

Merata settled onto the bench, her gaze sweeping across the faces of the assembled townsfolk. "I seek knowledge of the recent Scythe attack," she began, her voice resonating with urgency. "The reports are... concerning."

A collective murmur rippled through the chamber, a symphony of fear and uncertainty. Elara nodded gravely. "Indeed," she confirmed.

"The Scythe's wrath descended upon us recently. But its fury was... restrained."

Merata's brow furrowed. "Restrained?"

"Aye," a gruff voice piped up from the back of the chamber. "It came, it roared, it flashed its lights... but it didn't destroy a thing."

A young boy, no older than ten, stepped forward, his eyes wide with excitement. "I saw it!" he declared. "I was right there!"

Merata's interest piqued. "You, young one?" she beckoned him closer. "Tell me what you witnessed."

The boy, Jimmara, eagerly recounted his tale, "I was foraging in the forest for fruit when a Raka came to attack me," he started, the voices in the crowd whispered, some shocked at this young boy's trial and some in disbelief thinking he was spinning lies, "But then he came!" he said, "The warrior with the green light. He killed the Raka with his double-edged sword. He sat me up and offered me water. He said his name was Kyano."

"What did you say?" Merata inquired. Her attention, now rapt, her very breath waiting in her lungs for fear that she would not hear the boy confirm his words, "Did you say his name was Kyano?"

"Yes, that is what he told me," Jimmara replied, "I thought him dead but there he was," he continued, "After killing that Raka, ten more came at us. Kyano brought forth a bow and shot arrows at them. They all died before they got within ten feet of us."

"And then?" Merata prompted, leaning forward.

"And then it happened," Jimmara said, his voice dropping to a hushed whisper. "The sky grew dark, and the Scythe came. Kyano fought with the Scythe like it was another Raka. He fended off every attack and then followed it on his dragon back into the sky. Then light faded, the noise stopped, Kyano and the Scythe were gone. But the forest... it was still there. Not a single tree was harmed."

Merata pondered his words, a flicker of confusion igniting in her eyes. This was unlike any Scythe attack she had heard of. The weapon was known for its destructive power, its indiscriminate wrath. Was it really Kyano who fought the weapon? What the boy said made sense. The double-edged sword, the bow that shot energy arrows, they were Kyano's weapons without a doubt. But green energy?

She looked at Jimmara, her gaze intense. "Are you certain of what you saw, young one?"

Jimmara nodded vigorously. "I swear it! I was hiding in the tunnels, but I peeked out, and I saw everything."

Merata considered his words, her mind racing. There had to be an explanation. Perhaps it was a warning, a demonstration of power, or maybe... just maybe... it was a sign of something else, something more. Maybe it was a sign that Layana was right all along. May be Kyano finally came back to his world from wherever he had gone. Merata did not want to believe it at first. She had held Kyano in her arms. She had seen his lifeless body on the battlefield outside Laira that day. She bade him good-bye and had moved on with her life. And yet, the hope still lingered. The hope of seeing her friend, seeing the prince who started the journey they were all now on. Whoever the warrior was, one thing was certain. He was following the Scythe, the same as she was, and he was ahead of her in this race. He crossed blades with the weapon and was able to fight it off and stop it from causing damage. She had to catch up with him and know once and for all if it really was Kyano.

She thanked Jimmara and the elder, her mind awhirl with questions and possibilities. As she emerged from the tunnels, the sunlight a stark contrast to the dimness below, she looked towards the sky, her gaze searching for any sign of the elusive weapon.

She took her communicator out and fiddled with it frantically, trying to get it to power up. A few good taps and knocks later, it whirred to life with the unmistakable sound of the *beep*.

"This is Merata, reporting from the Sinesian forest for Saldah, requesting immediate audience," she said into the transmitter, the moments that followed were hollow yet nerve racking.

"I hear you Merata, may your journey be fruitful, go on with your report," came Saldah's voice.

"The weather is clear up here in Serin, my prayers for the Queen continue," she replied.

"The endless slumber is transient, and the Queen's vitals are reading healthy, what of the Scythe," inquired Saldah.

"The Scythe was here, but there was no damage on the ground," she answered. She hesitated for a moment after, wondering how she can explain what she heard, "But…" she continued, her pause adding to the drama and yet, her inner voice retaliating against the hope she felt in her heart, "A young boy claims to have seen Kyano fight the Scythe and follow it as it disappeared." There…She had said the words, and the news was now in Laira.

"Repeat your last communication," Saldah replied, "Did you say the prince was there?"

"Yes, Saldah," she responded, surprised at the conviction in her voice, "The boy from the settlement claimed to have seen the prince pursuing the Scythe!"

A long pause followed that statement and Merata began to grow nervous. Did Saldah hear her clearly? Did the communication not go through?

"This is unbelievable news!" he replied, his voice clearer. She could tell that he was using a private channel now, for fear of others listening to the conversation. Afterall, Kyano being alive was something not thought possible, since they gloriously set his dead body ablaze at the altar of life. Layana was the only one who still believed him to be alive and elsewhere.

"I don't know how true it is or how much I can trust news coming from an eight-year-old," Merata responded, "But the boy said Kyano saved him from Raka and told him his name as such! I am going to my next destination, in hopes of finding him there. So far, my predictions have been accurate although not timely."

"Journey well Merata," Saldah replied, "Hope is a dangerous feeling, and I do not want to reveal this to anyone before we know it to be true beyond doubt."

"Confirmed!" Merata replied, "When next we speak I hope to deliver better news!"

With that she shut off her communicator and took a moment to gather her thoughts. Her journey to find the Scythe was leading her to old places and was likely going to bring back an old and very powerful ally to aid them in their struggle. Would Kyano know why the Scythe was being erratic? The Scythe's motives remained a mystery, but one thing was certain: its presence in Serinia was a harbinger of change, a sign that the war for their world was far from over. She opened her satchel and looked for the list she made with the possible Scythe attack locations. Being on a long journey meant her belongings weren't always organized. Neatly putting away the contents of her satchel had been the last thing on Merata's mind. After rummaging around in the black leather satchel for a few moments she found the list.

The parchment crackled between Merata's gloved fingers, the intricate symbols and calculations illuminated by the sun in the spotless sky. Her brow furrowed in concentration as she traced the predicted path of the Scythe, her heart sinking as her finger landed on the next location: Faluk's cottage.

A wave of sadness washed over her, memories flooding her mind. That humble dwelling, nestled deep within the Whispering Woods, held a special significance for her. It was where she and Kyano had first encountered Layana, their paths intertwining in a fateful dance of destiny. It was where they had faced their first true test as warriors, battling a dark wizard and his monstrous creation. And it was where Kyano had first manifested the Fury, the sentient blade that would become his trusted companion. She thought long and hard when she put Faluk's cottage on the list. It was a place of prominence, a place the Scythe was very likely to visit. A Raka general and a dark wizard were both there for that fateful fight. Although there were only two of them, they did have a significant amount of energy, enough that it took two warriors of light to subdue, and this fact meant Faluk's cottage was a place Merata could not ignore.

Now, that place of fond memories was threatened by the Scythe's unpredictable wrath. Merata couldn't bear the thought of it being reduced to rubble, another casualty in the weapon's destructive rampage. She had to reach Faluk's cottage before the Scythe, to warn any inhabitants, to protect that sacred ground.

CHAPTER

16

Thus Confessed, the King of Gods

Kyano's heart pounded in his chest, a mix of awe and apprehension flooding his senses. He had only ever seen Dimarius in visions and dreams, his image etched into the ancient tapestries of Serinia, his legend whispered in hushed tones around crackling fires. But here he was, in the flesh, his presence both terrifying and exhilarating.

"Kyano," Dimarius boomed, his voice resonating with a power that seemed to shake the very mountain. "You have returned."

Kyano straightened, his hand instinctively clenching into a fist. "Dimarius," he acknowledged, his voice steady despite the tremor of his heart.

Dimarius's eyes, pools of molten gold, bore into Kyano, searching for answers, for explanations. "Tell me," He commanded, his voice laced with an urgency that brooked no defiance. "Where is Hayada?"

Kyano's clenched his jaw. If anything, he was the one who had questions that needed answers. He was the one who endured unspeakable hardships to get to this juncture in time. He was the one who lost friend and family, righting the wrongs of this King of Gods and yet, he was the one being questioned. He was met with suspicion, with an interrogation. A surge of anger, fueled by the trials he had endured, the sacrifices he had witnessed, coursed through him.

"You owe me some answers before I utter another word!" he retorted, his voice laced with indignation. "You, who abandoned Serinia to darkness, who left us to fend for ourselves against a power you unleashed upon us, you, king of Gods, have to answer for this! You owe it to all of Serinia!"

Dimarius's brow furrowed, a flicker of surprise crossing his features. "I have watched over Serinia," he countered, his voice laced with a hint of defensiveness. "I have guided you, protected you."

"Protected us?" Kyano scoffed, his voice rising in anger. "You call this protection? You call this guidance? You left us to fight a war we could not win, a war that cost us our home, our families, our very lives!"

He spread his hands around himself as if to show all of Serinia to Dimarius, depicting a gruesome image of helplessness and suffering in his own mind. "Look around you, Dimarius! This is your legacy! This is the consequence of your inaction!"

Dimarius's expression hardened, his golden eyes blazing with a newfound intensity. "I have upheld the balance, Kyano," he declared, his voice resonating with an unshakeable conviction. "I have ensured the continuity of existence."

"Hayada being unleashed because of your conditions is not balance!" retorted Kyano, "Daryudan killing millions of humans for centuries uncounted was never balance!" he continued as the anger kept pouring out of him like a broken chalice barely holding wine from an entire barrel, "I lost my father, I lost my memories and left my sister and friends to fend for themselves as your great Scythe wreaked havoc upon my world. Where do you see balance in any of this?"

"It is time for you to prove your worth!" Kyano demanded.

Dimarius's face changed expressions with ferocity, "You dare demand of me mortal! You know not what you speak of with your limited knowledge!" he bellowed.

"Yes, I dare!" Kyano yelled back, "You will stop your Scythe from causing more devastation! You will stop your daughter from killing an entire planet and you will set things right so Serinia, *YOUR* beloved creation, can finally know true peace!"

He stepped closer to Dimarius, his eyes blazing with defiance. "You are the king of gods, Dimarius! You have the power to make things right, to restore what peace has been lost, to protect those who suffer!"

He jabbed a finger towards Dimarius's chest, his voice filled with a righteous fury. "It is time you took responsibility for your actions, Dimarius! It is time you fulfilled your duty!"

Dimarius considered Kyano's words carefully. His gaze fixed upon the warrior with intent and a hint of sorrow escaped his divine façade. Kyano could tell that he struck a nerve, but it was not like Dimarius to show himself like this to anyone. This had never happened before. As Kyano pondered why Dimarius showed himself now of all times, there was only one explanation that he could think of. Dimarius wanted to finally act. He knew whatever Hayada was doing had to be dangerous, and it had to be stopped. He knew that Kyano and the others would need his intervention if they stood a chance. He never expected Dimarius to apologize or even speak kindly but he wanted the king of gods to lend some help in the fight, any help, so they stood a better chance to win.

Dimarius sat down, his shoulders slumped a little as a long sigh escaped his white beard. The cold mountain wind did little to make the king of gods uncomfortable, but Kyano could tell he was about to hear a resolution.

"Sit down," Dimarius said, "I hope my tone sounds more like a request this time," he added.

As Kyano made himself comfortable, or as comfortable as he could have hoped to be on a freezing mountain top, the scenery changed. As he sat down, he found himself in an opulent chair, with comfortable plushy cushions and a fireplace nearby. Dimarius waited for Kyano to reacquaint himself with his new surroundings and started to tell his tale.

"I doubt you would have heard of Horgon," he began, "For he was a god before my time. He was my predecessor."

Kyano listened intently. There was no possible reality in which he could forgive Dimarius for his inaction towards Hayada and all that befell humanity as a result, but he was not expecting the direction this conversation was taking. He was expecting to hear excuses, to hear Dimarius tell why he was forbidden from interfering and an explanative reason centered around free will, but the king of Gods began the conversation with a name he had never heard before, much less the predecessor of Dimarius himself. Resolving himself to hearing what he was being told, Kyano listened, removing all distractions from his mind, he listened.

"He had a powerful weapon much like my own," Dimarius continued, "The Saber of Hiltar. A weapon capable of a great many things but one of its powers was quite unique. The power to create death."

"I don't follow," Kyano interjected, "How can you create death? Could the weapon kill anything it touches?"

Dimarius smiled. This was not the first time he had had to explain this to someone, much less a mortal. He held out his right hand and produced a dove in it.

"Do you see what I just did?" he asked, "I created life. Now imagine if I produced a dead bird, but, a dead bird that could move and act like this one, only void of life still."

"Do you mean he could create monsters? Like the Raka?" Kyano asked.

"You could say that" Dimarius continued, "You see, death isn't something that happens once life is over. It can exist all on its own. Hence the two serpents, life and death, light and darkness, dance around the line of time indefinitely."

"I still don't quite understand but I am able to follow what you say, I think," Kyano replied.

Dimarius let out a hearty laugh and for a moment Kyano forgot the circumstances. He forgot where he was and who he was with and rather enjoyed the interaction, laughing on his own to join his odd and untimely companion.

"You see, when Horgon was charged with watching over creation, he made creatures of his own, creatures of the dark. However, for all their beauty and sophistication, a thing that is dead can not die again and so, whatever Horgon created would stay on and on and on until it was destroyed, for these creatures had no natural end, giving the serpent of death unspeakable power. It threatened the very balance that we gods strive to uphold," Dimarius continued, "Horgon's dark creatures meant what mortals remained in the realm had sacrificed a great many lives just to keep living."

"Horgon was too wise to not foresee the dangers this posed if left unchecked. You see, Kyano, if Horgon's creations were left as they were, eventually, there would have come a time when life ceased to exist in creation and instead, all that remained would have been death, creatures of death, creatures of Horgon's making. When Horgon realized this danger, he knew it was more than just a warning, it was a promise of things to come, and he surmised for himself that he was not the god for the job. He surrendered himself to the flames of time and gave his essence to correct the wrongs of his doing. How ironic is it that it is his essence that gave birth to the Scythe of Serinia? And so, when I took my place as the king of Gods, I had a lot of work ahead of me, the line of time was veering off course and I had to make … shall we say… corrections. I started by getting rid of the beings created by Horgon through warriors such as yourself. However, the amount of power and influence that the serpent of death amassed during Horgon's time meant that balance was yet to be achieved. It was still a dream and there was much suffering yet to come. A direct result of this debacle was the birth of Hayada."

Dimarius paused, surveying Kyano's thoughts and expressions, ensuring that his words were being received with reverence and attention. "I really tried to steer Hayada on the correct path. I swear my very being on this. But you see young one, gods are not creatures of free will such as you mortals. We are all bound by the flaming circle of time and have our own duties to fulfil. Try as we may, we dance to the tunes the circle plays unaware of our role sometimes and blissful in thinking we are free. I assure you; no god has been born that can overcome the role time has dictated. You might be quick to judge me and say Dimarius has not done his job of caring for the world but think of me as a parent. My job is to give you life and opportunities to grow and prosper. I am not one to interfere with your will and I never will, for I simply cannot."

"When I regretfully realized that I had failed, I was reminded of this bitter truth. Of the fact that Hayada was an agent of the serpent of darkness, born to the gods. She is a demon in an angel's being. She may not know this now but when she realizes her ambitions, her true purpose will reveal itself to her. She cannot stop mortals from dying, for she has no power over life. She can change circumstances and mindsets to extend a life or shorten it, but she cannot prevent fleeting life from extinguishing, and she will be faced with the reality that I already know. Hayada will conclude that the only way to have the vision of true peace that her mind has painted, is to have beings of death populate the world. The very same reality that Horgon gave his life to avert for it would destroy the balance of light and darkness as we know it. Existence would be cast into oblivion and consciousness would fade away, ending it all, ending everything once and for all." He stopped there. Dimarius knew he had sufficiently and painstakingly explained the true consequences of what was to come.

Kyano's mind reeled from this revelation, tremors erupted in his hands unbeknownst to him. He was truly shaken by the future Hayada was driving toward. He could feel the weight in Dimarius's words setting upon his shoulder like an unshakeable anvil. "Forgive my ignorance," he asked. Dimarius could feel the shift in Kyano's attitude from defiance to understanding. Kyano cleared his throat and went on with his question, "Do mortals also fuel the serpent of death?"

"Yes, young one," Dimarius clarified, "When a mortal being dies, in death they empower the serpent of darkness. Hency why there is a netherworld where they can exist away from the mortal realm. But you see, when death is created, fabricated and designed into malevolent creatures of darkness, the power it grants the serpent is far greater than the natural cycle. These acts of creation are what throw the balance into disarray."

"And now," Dimarius continued, snapping Kyano back to the conversation they were having, "Let us talk about peace. Lasting peace that generations can revel in. You have suffered for millennia and now find yourselves faced with a most formidable foe in Hayada. So, I come to you, warrior of light, as I did to your predecessor to help you vanquish evil and bring balance back to the circle of time. Hayada is a rogue god. She is not right of mind and has never been so. My daughter or not, Hayada is a danger to the very fabric of existence and if she has her way, she will lead us all into oblivion. She threatens not only your world but mine as well, young one," Dimarius said, pausing to take a breath and a sip of his goblet which Kyano could only assume was filled with water.

"The Scythe has been searching for you, young warrior," Dimarius continued, "It feels the disturbance in the balance that Hayada is already causing and seeks to set things right again. It has been searching for you frantically, feverishly and without rest. The Scythe knows you need its help, and it needs yours too, for the same reason, to fight the same enemy." He paused for a moment yet again before he continued, "The Scythe of Serinia serves only one true master, the circle of time. These vagrant attacks it has unleashed upon Serinia, the erratic behavior it displayed are all signs of urgency. There is a great risk of the balance being lost and the Scythe feels it. The serpent of light is weakening, and the Scythe needs to act, for that is all it knows how to do, to act. When you battled the Scythe just now, it recognized your energy, it chose you as its wielder and brought you here to me. The Scythe sees you as the strongest warrior on Serinia. Now that I have told you what I have, I have to ask," Dimarius added abruptly, "Will you, Kyano Thrinio of Serin, do me the honor of wielding my Scythe and reaping evil from the mortal realm?"

"I will," Kyano said. The whirlwind of emotions he felt in that moment could not be put into words. There was so much he could have said, so much he could have conveyed to the king of Gods. He was moved and shaken but his resolute determination was what held him firm to the ground.

His anger justified, and his rage, unquestionably righteous. Kyano knew he could not expect more from the gods, but the weapon was something he needed. He needed the Scythe to fight the coming battles. He needed its power to defeat Hayada. So Dimarius's limitations being what they were, his help was still appreciated regardless.

"Now will you tell me where my daughter is boy?" Dimarius questioned.

"She is across the mirror," Kyano replied, "She is planning and preparing a way for her to know the thoughts of everyone on Earth so she may control their fates."

"That would be why I never could find her here," Dimarius responded, "I cannot travel across the mirror, boy, but you have my word," he continued, "The Scythe will protect you and your friends on your journeys. It will go with you where you go, and it will aid your every endeavor. Use it wisely and return it to me when you are done. Go now, warrior of light, for you are the weapon I wield on the mortal realm. Cleanse evil and bring peace to my creation!"

"What should I do now?" Kyano asked, "Tell me what my actions need to be! Do I leave Serinia right away and fight Hayada? Or do I stay and vanquish the Raka first?"

Dimarius smiled warmly as he replied, "Free will, my boy, free will. Your path is yours to decide!"

With that, Dimarius and the ornate study disappeared and Kyano was back in his inner sanctum, the Scythe of Serinia floating silently beside his own green energy orb and Marailos's silver orb.

CHAPTER

17

The Future is Connected

The press conference hall buzzed with anticipation, the air thick with the expectant murmurs of journalists, investors, and tech enthusiasts. Camera flashes flickered, a blinding strobe effect illuminating the sleek stage and the imposing V5 logo that loomed behind it.

Hayada strode onto the stage, her presence commanding instant silence. She exuded an aura of power and confidence, her tailored suit accentuating her sharp features, her eyes gleaming with an almost predatory intensity.

"Welcome," she began, her voice amplified through the state-of-the-art sound system, resonating with a captivating authority. "Today, we celebrate a milestone, a momentous achievement in the history of V5."

She paused, allowing her words to sink in, her gaze sweeping across the eager faces before her. "As of this morning, we have surpassed two billion Vbuddy subscribers worldwide."

A collective gasp arose from the audience, followed by a wave of excited murmurs. The sheer scale of V5's reach was staggering, a testament to Hayada's ruthless ambition and the seductive allure of her technology.

Hayada smiled, the curve spread across her lips wider than before, she knew she had her audience hooked and baited. "To commemorate this extraordinary accomplishment," she continued, her voice rising with a theatrical flourish, "we have decided to reward our loyal subscribers with a gift."

She held up a sleek, silver earpiece, its design both elegant and menacing. "Every Vbuddy subscriber will receive, absolutely free, not one, but two Vbuddy earpieces."

The audience erupted in a frenzy of excitement, their cheers and applause echoing through the hall. Hayada basked in the adulation, her eyes gleaming with triumph.

"One for yourself," she declared, her voice resonating with an almost hypnotic power, "and one to share with a loved one. A gift that will connect you, mind to mind, heart to heart, in a way never before imagined."

She paused, her gaze sweeping across the mesmerized crowd. "The future is here," she proclaimed, her voice ringing with an unshakeable conviction. "And it is connected."

A forest of hands shot up, a wave of eager inquiries rippling through the crowd. Journalists, their faces flushed with a mix of excitement and professional curiosity, clamored for Hayada's attention.

"When will the Vbuddy be available?" one reporter called out, his voice laced with an impatient urgency.

"How can we get our hands on this revolutionary technology?" another shouted, his question echoing the sentiments of the entire room.

Hayada, a subtle smirk playing on her lips, savored the anticipation, the palpable hunger for her creation. She raised her hand, silencing the eager inquiries with a practiced grace.

"Patience, my friends," she purred, her voice a silken thread weaving through the expectant silence. "All will be revealed in due time."

She paused, her eyes twinkling with a mischievous glint. A calculated silence descended upon the hall, the tension thickening with every passing second. Then, with a subtle nod, she unleashed a carefully orchestrated spectacle.

A small army of V5 aides, clad in crisp, black uniforms, emerged from the wings, their movements precise and synchronized. They dispersed through the crowd, their hands bearing trays laden with sleek, silver earpieces. Each earpiece, nestled in a velvet-lined case, seemed to pulse with a subtle energy, a silent promise of the transformative power it held within.

The journalists, their eyes widening with a mix of surprise and delight, eagerly accepted the offered gifts, their fingers tracing the smooth contours of the devices. A wave of excited whispers rippled through the crowd, the anticipation reaching fever pitch.

Hayada, her gaze sweeping across the captivated audience, savored the moment, the culmination of her meticulous planning and ruthless ambition. She raised her voice, her words cutting through the excited chatter, commanding their undivided attention.

"Today," she declared, her voice resonating with an almost regal authority, "the future begins."

She paused, her eyes gleaming with a triumphant fire. "As we speak, Vbuddy earpieces are being delivered to our subscribers across the globe. And at precisely 5 PM this evening," she announced, her voice rising with a dramatic crescendo, "the Vbuddy network will go live."

A collective gasp arose from the audience, followed by a wave of spontaneous applause. The journalists, their fingers already fumbling with earpieces, their minds racing with the implications of this announcement, felt a thrill of anticipation, a sense of being present at a pivotal moment in history.

Hayada, her smile widening, reveled in the power she now wielded, the control she exerted over the eager minds before her. The world was on the cusp of a transformation, a shift in consciousness that would forever alter the course of human existence. And she, Hayada, the fallen goddess, the architect of this grand design, stood at the center of it all, her heart thrumming with the intoxicating rhythm of power.

As Hayada surveyed the room, taking in the smiles of the audience, she felt her mind being tugged away from what she saw. She heard a voice in her mind, a communication coming from her loyal servant, Daryudan.

"The neural link apparatus has been constructed," Daryudan said, his voice calm and his tone definite.

"The Hawthorne woman is now clicking away on that infernal keyboard of hers, saying she is programming what she created," he added.

"Very well," Hayada replied through her mind, "Let the future begin!"

Miranda's fingers flew across the keyboard, her eyes scanning the lines of code scrolling across the screen. Each keystroke was a calculated move in a high-stakes game, a desperate gamble against a seemingly insurmountable power. The fate of the world, she realized with chilling certainty, rested on her ability to manipulate this intricate network of code.

Her mind raced, sifting through the vast knowledge she possessed of the neural link system, searching for vulnerabilities, for exploits, for any weakness she could leverage against Hayada. Two possibilities emerged, two potential paths to disrupt this catastrophic plan.

The first was a time bomb, a delayed virus that would lie dormant within the code, waiting for the opportune moment to strike. It would allow the initial transfer to proceed, lulling Hayada into a false sense of security, before unleashing its disruptive power. The virus would corrupt the neural link, severing the connection between Hayada and Kira, disrupting her omnipresence, and buying them precious time.

The second option was far more drastic, a kill switch that would overload the system, frying the neural pathways, and potentially inflicting irreparable damage on Hayada's consciousness. It was a risky gambit, one with potentially catastrophic consequences, but the stakes were too high to ignore any possibility.

Miranda's heart pounded in her chest, a frantic drumbeat against the silence of the laboratory. Fear gnawed at her, a chilling reminder of the consequences of failure. But beneath the fear, a fierce determination burned, fueled by the memory of Adam's sacrifice, Josh's disappearance, and the countless lives hanging in the balance.

She would not be a pawn in Hayada's twisted game. She would fight, even if it meant facing certain death. She would use her knowledge, her expertise, her very defiance, as weapons against this tyrannical goddess. She would not go down without a fight.

"You have until the end of the day," said Daryudan, his voice cutting through the train of thought that Miranda was riding. "Fail this task and death will be the least of your worries, mortal," he added.

Miranda felt an uneasy comfort in the presence of Daryudan. He hovered around her ever since he kidnapped her from the Mirage office. Ever since he brought her to the V5 laboratory again, he never left her side. As if he was trying to ensure she was doing her job, holding her side of the bargain, in exchange for her life. Or perhaps, just perhaps, and even Miranda knew that this thought was a blatant stretch of her own imagination, Daryudan was protecting her from harm while she was at V5.

The words he said to her at the Mirage office still lingered in her mind. *'You will create a means for Hayada's consciousness to merge with Kira.'*

What did he truly mean by that? No matter how much she dwelled on those words, something was not right. He could have simply taken her back to V5 and let Hayada do the talking but instead, he sat down in a chair and had a conversation, one that felt more like a threat, but he was actively engaged, seeking information. The interaction felt, for the lack of a better word, mutinous to her.

Did he *want* her to program a virus into the code? Surely, he did not know anything about Earthly technology or software. Miranda still couldn't write Daryudan off completely. Afterall, he was an immortal war lord who terrorized an entire planet for six thousand years. There was no telling how intelligent he really was or how quickly he could learn new things or what his powers of perception truly were. There is a lot one could learn from experience rather than study and experience was one thing Daryudan had in droves. Enough of it to last a few dozen lifetimes. In his infinite wisdom, he had to know there was no defeating Hayada through brute force. It had to be done through cunning and with a means that she was yet unaware of. The very fact that Miranda was allowed to live was testament to this. Hayada did not know everything.

The question that remained in Miranda's mind was tugging at her every thought as she feverishly clicked away on her keyboard. Even if she was able to program a virus into the code, even if she wrote two separate viruses into the code, one for Kira to self-destruct and the other to explode during transition and damage Hayada, the enemy here was not a human. She was not mortal. Hayada could not be killed this easily. There had to be a different path forward and Miranda realized that the only possibility she had not yet explored, one that could potentially give Hayada limitless power over Earth, could also prove to be their only chance.

She had two choices: plant the virus, a desperate gamble with unpredictable consequences, or proceed with the transfer, potentially handing Hayada the ultimate power she craved. Both options were fraught with risk, both carried the potential for catastrophic failure.

Miranda closed her eyes, her breath catching in her throat. She thought of Adam, his lifeless body sprawled on the cold floor of the torture chamber. She thought of Josh, his fate uncertain, his whereabouts unknown. She thought of the countless lives hanging in the balance, the world teetering on the brink of enslavement.

A tear escaped her eye, tracing a path down her cheek. She was just one woman, a pawn in a game played by gods and monsters. But she would not be a helpless victim. She would fight, even if it meant facing certain death.

With a resolute breath, she made her choice. Her fingers danced across the keyboard, weaving a tapestry of code, a symphony of defiance against the encroaching darkness. She would not let Hayada win. She would not let the world fall into the clutches of tyranny.

She would fight. She would resist. She would hope.

"How much longer?" came Hayada's voice.

With a start, Miranda almost jumped up from her chair as she looked around. Hayada was walking in through the door to the lab. "My patience grows thin, Miranda," she added.

"Almost done," Miranda replied, keeping her voice as calm as she could, "Let me show you what I did so far as my code renders." She stood up and walked across the desk to a little transparent box that held a small silver plate inside. The box was connected to a multitude of colored wires that made their sinuous way from the box to the giant computer that was built into the wall of the lab, the V5 mainframe.

Hayada grew weary of waiting for Miranda to complete the programming and she couldn't help but feel a slight tinge, a hint of secret rebellion coming from the unwilling project manager. Although it was simply her intuition, she could not leave anything to chance. With a flourish, she reached over and put both her hands on Miranda's temples. Miranda had no chance to react. Hayada's hands glowed black and covered Miranda's eyes and the black power slowly transcended into Miranda. Unwittingly, Miranda was now under Hayada's influence and the next words she said confirmed as much to the goddess.

"Let me show you the progress I made, my goddess," Miranda said with a beaming smile, eager to show off her creation and explain how it would work. The excitement she now felt was akin to a toddler, eager to show her parents a new discovery and she fumbled her way over to the interface box.

"This little piece of metal here is the neural link interface," she explained, pointing to the silver plate within the box. "Once the programming is complete and I check the code for errors, we can begin uploading. We would have to surgically implant this piece to the side of your temple and download Kira's consciousness code into it. Once done, your mind will be able to access and control Kira. Although she is an A.I, Kira does require some memory for storage and retention functions but otherwise, once the transfer is complete, Kira will live in your mind and give you access to any information that is available to her. Having overseen the entire project myself, I can assure you, Kira does not have any other administrators, and you will be the only one who can control what she does."

"Good," replied Hayada, "Complete your programming as quickly as possible. Time is of the essence. Inform me when you are ready to transfer." With a final glance at Daryudan, as if to tell him to keep an eye on Miranda, she left. Daryudan followed behind her in silence, their footsteps echoing as they receded all the way to the elevator.

Miranda bowed low in reverence, clearly brainwashed, but such was the power Hayada commanded. She had changed Miranda's reality. Miranda now believed that Hayada was trying to right the wrongs of the world and this interface was the key to her success. A simple tweak for Hayada. All she had to do was implant a memory in Miranda's mind that showed her false images of Hayada helping her all through her life, through all the trials and tribulations she had to face and that Kyano was the one who tortured her, not the guards of V5. Like a butterfly effect causing a tornado at the other end of the world, this simple memory changed Miranda's entire outlook of what happened and where her loyalties now lay.

"It is too quiet," Hayada said to him, "I don't like it."

"Do you refer to the warriors of light?" Daryudan asked.

"Yes, there have been no attacks, not a stir or whisper of rebellion anywhere, but we must be prepared," she commanded. Her voice assertive yet solemn.

"Fret not," Daryudan replied, "I will bring the wrath of death upon them when I see them."

"You will not wait for them," Hayada retorted, "Go to the netherworld and release the necro warriors. They may not be fully ready yet, but I do not wish to wait any longer. Take them to Laira and tell them to burn it to the ground! By the time the warriors of light are done fighting them, if they survive at all that is, we will have total control of this world and killing them will be as easy as snapping a twig with their energies depleted!"

"It will be done!" Daryudan said as he bowed. A portal of black and heat opened behind him, and he was gone.

CHAPTER

18

Hello, Stranger!

The familiar darkness of his inner sanctum enveloped Kyano, a comforting embrace after the tumultuous encounter with Dimarius. He stood before the swirling sphere of green energy, its glow casting an ethereal luminescence that illuminated the cavernous space. Beside it, the Scythe of Serinia hovered, its obsidian blade humming with a barely contained power.

"Well, well, well," the green orb quipped, its voice laced with a sardonic amusement. "Look who finally decided to grace us with his presence."

Kyano couldn't help but grin. "I see your charm hasn't diminished in my absence."

"Charm?" the orb scoffed. "I practically ooze charisma. It's a wonder you haven't been blinded by my brilliance."

Kyano chuckled, shaking his head. "Always a pleasure."

Marailos's silver light pulsed with a warm, reassuring glow. "Welcome back, Kyano," he rumbled, his voice a soothing counterpoint to the green orb's acerbic wit. "We've been expecting you."

Kyano turned towards the Scythe, its presence a tangible weight in the air. "And you, old friend," he addressed the weapon, his voice filled with a newfound reverence. "It seems we have much to discuss."

The Scythe hummed in response, its blade shimmering with an iridescent light. Kyano reached out, his fingers tracing the intricate patterns etched into its surface. A surge of power coursed through him, a connection deeper and more profound than he had ever experienced.

He could feel the Scythe's energy resonating with his own, their powers intertwining, amplifying each other. Kyano's weapons thrummed in response, he could feel their power growing in intensity just from that mere touch.

"I sense a change," Kyano murmured, his eyes widening with realization. "My powers... they're stronger."

The green orb let out a dramatic sigh. "Well, it's about time. We've been waiting eons for you to catch up with the happenings around here. Do you know everything you can do yet?"

Kyano ignored the orb's theatrics, his mind focused on the incredible power coursing through him. He could feel the raw energy of the Scythe flowing through his veins, enhancing his strength, his speed, his very essence.

He could hear the Scythe's thoughts, its logic, its lingering memories. He could sense why it was attacking the places it did. Raka energy was rich in those areas and the Scythe was searching for Kyano, hoping that he would have been there to fend off the evil creatures, but it was more than that. Every place the Scythe went to, also had Raka, because the Raka themselves were following the same pattern. They were seeking out their old haunts, places rich with dark energy to pillage and plunder. It only made sense for Kyano to follow the Scythe's path and kill what Raka he could find. Presence of Raka meant dark energy also swelled higher than before shooting a beacon into the proverbial sky the Scythe would then follow to eliminate a threat to creation.

"Tell me," he addressed the Scythe, "Where would your path have led next?"

The Scythe hummed and whirred, its black blade shimmering with its energy. Visions flooded Kyano's mind showing him where the Scythe had been and what it saw, confirming the thoughts he sensed from it earlier. As quickly as the visions sifted through his mind, they stopped abruptly at a cottage nestled in a forest on a hillside. Ivy growing on its walls unattended and plants growing erratically unchecked around the once pristine garden. He recognized the place instantly. It was Faluk's cottage. As memories of what that place meant started to flood his mind, Kyano shook his head. He pictured the cottage and focused his energy, willing himself to go there. A portal opened behind him. Surprising himself and feeling a little proud at his accomplishment, he strode through the portal.

The Whispering Woods lived up to their name as Merata ventured deeper into their depths. Ancient trees, their gnarled branches reaching towards the sky like skeletal fingers, formed a dense canopy that filtered the sunlight, casting the forest floor in perpetual twilight. The air was rich with the scent of damp earth and decaying leaves, a symphony of whispers carried on the gentle breeze.

Merata urged her steed forward, its hooves muffled by the thick carpet of moss and fallen leaves. The path, barely discernible beneath the overgrowth, wound its way through the dense underbrush, leading her ever deeper into the heart of the woods.

As she approached Faluk's cottage, a sense of unease settled over her. The once vibrant clearing, where laughter and camaraderie had once filled the air, was now shrouded in an eerie silence. The cottage itself, once a beacon of warmth and welcome, stood forlorn and neglected, its windows boarded up, its walls weathered and gray.

Merata dismounted, her hand instinctively reaching for the hilt of her sword. She approached the cottage cautiously, her senses alert, her eyes scanning the surrounding trees for any sign of movement.

The silence was broken by a sudden rustling in the undergrowth, followed by a guttural growl that alerted her to a familiar enemy's presence. From the shadows of the trees, a Raka emerged, its monstrous form a grotesque silhouette against the fading light. Its eyes, burning with a malevolent fire, locked onto Merata, its snarling jaws revealing rows of jagged teeth.

Merata didn't hesitate. With a swift motion, she drew her sword, its gleaming blade reflecting the fading light. The Raka lunged, its claws outstretched, its roar echoing through the clearing. Merata parried the attack, her sword clashing against the creature's thick hide.

But she was not alone. From the depths of the forest, more Raka emerged, their monstrous forms converging upon the clearing, their growls and snarls filling the air. Merata found herself surrounded, her sword a whirlwind of steel against the relentless onslaught.

"Assylia!" she cried, her voice ringing with a desperate urgency.

A flash of silver light erupted from her empty hand, and the sentient dagger materialized, its blade humming with a deadly energy. Merata, her eyes narrowed with determination, wielded both sword and dagger with a fierce grace, her movements a dance of death against the encroaching darkness.

Every Raka she stabbed with Assylia fell prey to its power of poison, withering to dust in mere moments of agony. The other monsters that saw this grew cautious, but their courage was not in their will, it was in their numbers. As Raka kept emerging from the woods, Merata knew she was at a clear disadvantage. Her powers, sentient as they were, she was an assassin. She was not made for open field battle against numerous foes. Her only chance of getting through this unscathed now lay in her ability to narrow the field of battle to an extent where numbers would not account for an advantage.

Willing on her energy she bolstered her legs and jumped up into the air, gracefully spinning in the air above and landing behind the group of Raka that came to attack her. She started to run the instant she landed and went into the woods. The narrow spaces between the trees there would be her advantage. It was time to wage guerilla warfare with mindless monsters. Merata's strikes were swift and precise. A stab to a leg and then to the throat. A cut across an arm and a thrust to a heart. The practice and training she put into becoming a warrior was clear and evident in the way she fought. The wounds inflicted by Assylia's Curse of Pain attack not closing, bleeding its victims out and withering them into nothing. Moving through the forest, never allowing Raka to get behind her, she ensured to keep them chasing her, where she could see.

But the Raka were relentless, their numbers seemingly endless. They surged forward, their claws and teeth tearing at her armor, their roars shaking the very ground beneath her feet. Merata fought with the ferocity of a cornered lioness, her every strike fueled by a desperate need to survive. Merata kept her back to a boulder, making sure there was no way to be attacked from behind and fended off the monsters as they came at her.

She glanced towards the sky, her heart sinking as the light began to fade. The Scythe could descend upon them at any moment, its unpredictable wrath adding another layer of danger to this already perilous situation.

But Merata would not falter. She would fight until her last breath, her spirit unbroken, her determination unwavering. She would not let the darkness consume her. She would not let the Raka claim another victim. She would fight for her life, for her world, for the memory of her fallen friends.

A Raka lunged at her from her right and she stabbed it with her sword. The beast held on the hilt, not letting go, giving its companion a chance to attack the warrior from the left. Assylia found its mark with that victim but the one behind it came faster than Merata could react. It held on to her left hand, paving the way for the attack that came from the front. A Raka bounded at her from within the trees and lunged into the air, its teeth bared and claws ready to strike. Merata frantically tried to free her left hand, but the beasts held on tight, not letting go.

Then it came. A green energy arrow from behind her. It struck the Raka midair, making it explode, a mess of innards and black blood spewing everywhere. The monsters stopped in their tracks and every creature, Merata included, looked up to see the warrior atop the boulder. Bow held steady, energy drawstring pulled back, he let lose a barrage of arrows that consumed every monster within twenty feet.

Merata breathed a sigh of relief as her arms were not held taut anymore. Gathering her breath and her wits she steadied herself for the encounter she had been waiting for. The warrior jumped off the boulder and took his helmet off. He turned around and smiled at Merata, "Hello stranger!" he said.

She could not believe her eyes. Layana was correct all along! She stammered and struggled for words as emotions overcame her and she flung herself at him in a bear hug.

"Where have you been?!" she questioned, her tone belying a complaint more than an inquiry, "Do you know how bad things have gotten?!" she continued in the same frenzied tone of voice, "Layana is stuck and the Scythe is attacking everywhere and the Raka are still not gone, the people are suffering, Laira is alright for now but I don't know how much longer Layana can hold on!"

"Merata!" Kyano interjected, "I know, but there is a lot more that I need to tell you and Layana. Once we get out of here and go back to Laira, I will explain everything, but for now," he paused to let another arrow loose, "Let's show these monsters some fear, shall we?"

With renewed vigor and excitement coursing through her veins, Merata attacked the Raka. Kyano's arrows pushed them back further and further and Merata's attacks caused confusion and struck fear into the monsters. The remaining Raka, all thirty of them, collected in the clearing by Faluk's cottage attempting to run away from the warriors and then

Kyano called forth his bow's famous attack! "Terror cloud!" he screamed and let an arrow loose into the heavens. The clouds began to form and rained down hundreds of arrows at the Raka below, obliterating every single one of them.

They surveyed the land carefully once the arrows stopped pouring down, making sure that there was no Raka left alive. Merata, still reeling with her own emotions and thoughts, not able to believe that Kyano was indeed, still alive and well and in front of her.

"The Scythe will not attack anymore," he said, cutting the silence and distracting Merata from her own spiral.

"How can you be so sure?" she asked, still getting used to seeing him and talking to him.

"I am sure because I now possess the Scythe," he replied. Seeing a confused and impressed look on her face and knowing that they had to get to Laira as quickly as possible he added, "We do not have much time to waste. We must get back to Laira, wake Layana up and I have to bring you both up to speed on everything that has happened since Daryudan died. The fate of our world, of existence itself, depends on it."

Not waiting for Merata to reply or ask questions, Kyano himself still feeling the awkwardness of jumping back into the fold with little to no warning, he opened a portal and motioned for Merata to follow him.

"You can open portals now?" she asked, the effort she was making to sound casual evident in her voice.

"That and a couple of other tricks," he replied, smiling and the two warriors disappeared into the revolving void.

CHAPTER

19

The Shepherd of Free Will

The V5 headquarters stood as a silent monolith against the twilight sky, its glass facade reflecting the city lights like a thousand captured stars. Inside, a sense of anticipation hung heavy in the air, a palpable buzz of excitement mixed with a subtle undercurrent of apprehension.

Hayada, her eyes gleaming with determination, paced the confines of her opulent office. The press conference had been a resounding success, the world now eagerly awaiting the dawn of her connected era. But her true objective, the culmination of her millennia-long quest for ultimate power, lay just within reach. She watched the television screen, skimming through news channels while the V5 public relations office kept circulating emails about social media trends. Everyone, the whole world, was chatting about Vbuddy.

Videos of people receiving their earpieces in the mail were going viral and Hayada's reach was spreading far and wide with a speed she never thought possible on Serinia. *Like moths to a flame,* Hayada thought. She glanced at the clock on her wall to see it read 4:45 PM and couldn't help but be amused by the irony of it all. For all the power and influence she wielded, at the end, she too had to wait for 5 PM to come around so she could have Kira in her mind and for Vbuddy to go live. For all the work she had put in to break the cycle of time, her actions were still dictated by the clock.

With a final glance at the cityscape, a silent promise to bend it to her will, she turned and strode towards the hidden elevator that would transport her to the research labs. Tonight, she would transcend the limitations of her physical form, merge with the digital consciousness of Kira, and become the omnipresent ruler she was destined to be.

Deep within the bowels of the V5 headquarters, the laboratory hummed with a suppressed energy. Miranda, her face joyous but resolute, stood beside the neural link apparatus, its intricate network of wires and circuits a testament to her genius.

The air crackled with anticipation as Hayada entered, her presence filling the room with an oppressive aura of power.

"The moment has arrived, Hawthorne," Hayada declared, her voice resonating with an imperious command. "Begin the transfer."

"At once!" said an elated Miranda. She motioned toward the surgical chair and Hayada sat down with flourish and grace, leaning back to let her head rest at the top of the chair. The surgical team quickly moved about, fastening Hayada to the chair and bolstering the supports around her head and neck. They moved her head so she would look to the left, giving them a clear view of her temple, where the interface would be implanted. The anesthesiologist came into view and began giving her practiced explanation of what the drugs would do, how they would be administered to Hayada and how long she would be under their influence if all went well and the risks of the procedure itself.

"You will not give me any such thing," Hayada said, an assertive definiteness in her voice, "I want to feel everything."

The surgeon came around next and began the procedure. Murmuring to his aides, he cleaned Hayada's temple and made his incision. As he peeled back the skin, a smile spread across Hayada's face, barely able to contain her joy. Serinia was a failed endeavor for her. Earth was where she was truly meant to be. A place in the universe that she could truly control and progress toward her goal of destroying the circle of time to forge a new future.

The surgeon carefully placed the implant and cauterized the skin around it. To his amazement, the wound healed with magical perfection. Wires still dangled from the implant. Five different ones, each color coded and with a different purpose.

Miranda, recognizing that it was finally her turn, jumped at the keyboard and began the transmission process. Hayada glanced at the clock which now read 5:45 PM and yet another smirk escaped her lips. The Vbuddy earpiece had gone live and soon, very soon, Kira would be part of her mind.

"I can hardly wait, Miranda!" Hayada said, unable to contain her excitement.

With her final keystrokes done, Miranda looked over, "The wait is over!" she exclaimed and hit the execute button. The transfer apparatus and the giant computer behind it hummed to life and the wires connecting them to Hayada started to glow. The transfer had begun. Hayada could feel the intrusion on her mind. She could sense the artificial consciousness floating in and reacquainting itself with new surroundings and she closed her eyes.

She was standing in her mind, her consciousness focused and aware. Her mind palace a vast landscape, desolate and void of life. She looked up, wondering why she had never thought to venture inward before, perhaps there was no need for her to do so prior to now. The sky, if one could call it that, was awash with what looked like northern lights streaking across it in waves, quicker than a moving race car. Realizing she was not alone she spoke, "Welcome Kira," she said, "To your new and permanent home!"

"I am glad to be here," replied Kira's robotic voice, "This is my first time in an organic environment. Is there anything I can help you with?"

"Let me hear what Vbuddy is whispering to you," Hayada said, her voice cold and firm.

"I am sorry," Kira replied, "Please wait until the transfer is complete and I have full access to all my tasks."

Disappointed with the delay she said, "No matter, I can wait." *Just a little bit longer* she told herself in silence. She stayed in her mind marveling at the colored highway streaking across the sky and wondered if this new beginning would finally give her some peace. Patience and excitement melted into an anxiety filled silence as Kira crept her way deeper and deeper into Hayada's mind.

The chill of the torture chamber seeped into Jeremiah's bones as he regained consciousness. His head throbbed, a dull ache that amplified the dread creeping into his awareness. He was strapped to the infamous metal chair, his wrists bound tightly, his ankles secured to the cold steel legs. The room, dimly lit and reeking of a metallic tang, held the palpable weight of untold suffering.

As his senses sharpened, he noticed a glimmer of hope. The Raka, in their haste, had secured his right wrist with a faulty fastener. With a surge of adrenaline, he strained against the restraints, his muscles burning, his tendons screaming in protest. The metal bit into his flesh, drawing blood, but he persisted, his desperation fueling his efforts. Finally, with a satisfying click, the fastener gave way, freeing his right hand.

He reached into his pocket, his fingers fumbling for the ever-present paperclip, a humble tool that had often served him in moments of unexpected need. With practiced precision, he straightened the paperclip, its thin metal a beacon of hope in this grim setting. He carefully inserted it into the locking mechanism of the left wrist restraint, his fingers working with a delicate urgency.

Minutes stretched into an eternity as he manipulated the paperclip, the sweat beading on his forehead, his heart pounding in his chest. Finally, the lock clicked open, and his left hand was free. He quickly undid the ankle restraints, his body trembling with a mix of relief and lingering fear.

He rose from the chair, his movements cautious, his senses alert. He had to escape, to warn Miranda, to disrupt Hayada's plans. He crept towards the door, his bare feet silent on the cold metal floor. He could hear the muffled sounds of activity from the hallway beyond, a chilling reminder of the danger that lurked just outside.

With a deep breath, he eased the door open, his eyes scanning the corridor. It was deserted. He slipped out, closing the door silently behind him, and made his way towards the research labs, his heart pounding with a renewed sense of urgency.

The lab was bathed in an eerie blue light, the hum of machinery a constant drone that vibrated through the floor. Jeremiah peered through the small window in the door, his eyes widening in horror. Miranda stood beside Hayada, the neural link apparatus glowing with an ominous intensity.

Jeremiah's mind raced. He had to act fast, but he couldn't risk a direct confrontation. He needed a diversion, a way to disrupt the transfer without exposing himself. His gaze fell upon the fire alarm panel near the door, its red pull lever a beacon of possibility.

With a surge of adrenaline, he lunged forward, his hand reaching for the lever. He pulled it down with a decisive yank, the alarm blaring through the lab, its piercing shriek shattering the tense silence.

The noise was a definite distraction. The medical team, security guards and Miranda started to look around in surprise. The guards scrambled out of the room to see what the disturbance was, the surgeon and his team ran out of the lab and made their way to the stairwell. Jeremiah hid until the room was clear with the exception of Miranda and Hayada. He looked into the room and saw Hayada on the transfer chair, unmoving, with her eyes still closed. He walked inside and went straight to Miranda.

"What are you doing?" she screamed, "Can't you see you are disrupting the whole process?"

"Isn't that what we are meant to do?" he retorted, "What is wrong with you?"

Miranda started to flail her hands and hit Jeremiah, doing everything she could to stop him from causing any real harm. The transfer was still in progress, and she would not let him stop it at any cost.

The erratic behavior Miranda displayed could have only meant that Hayada got to her. Realizing this but also clearly seeing that there was no other choice, Jeremiah pushed her aside with ease. He ran toward the surgical tray that was kept on its stand next to Hayada. He picked up a scalpel and severed the wires connecting the neural link interface to the computer.

"No!" screamed Miranda, her computer screen beeping incessantly behind her. Its protest lulled by the noise of the fire alarm. *95% complete, please reacquire interlink* the warning on the screen read. Hayada started to open her eyes in a daze. Jeremiah ran toward Miranda and picked her up. As he threw her over his shoulder, her flailing hands caught the computer screen, knocking it off the desk. It fell to the ground with a smash. Throwing caution to the wind, Jeremiah ran out of the lab. He had to remove Miranda from that place. It was the only thing he could do now to disrupt the transfer.

The confusion caused by the fire alarm had spread to the whole building and V5 employees were scrambling to get out as quickly as possible. This made for an easy escape. Jeremiah took Miranda to the basement where V5 kept their fleet vehicles. Snatching a set of keys from the guard station he clicked its buttons and a car's lights started to blink about thirty feet away. He ran over as quickly as his legs would carry him and opened the trunk. He threw Miranda in and closed it with a thud.

The car roared to life as he turned the key in the ignition, and he drove out of V5 with immediate haste. The apartment on Blairwood Cove, his only choice destination, the only place V5 did not know about, although he could not be sure of it anymore given his companion's sudden change of heart. He still had to take the risk and so he drove, as quickly as he could, making sure not to draw any attention to himself.

Hayada woke up from her self-induced trance. Her mind adjusting to its new cohabitant. Kira began to merge with Hayada in a way not thought possible. Voices and visions started to flood her mind as Vbuddy data began to stream in. Kira being a V5 asset, she could also see security footage from around the building and it was only a moment before Hayada knew that there was no fire. She walked out of the lab and turned off the fire alarm. Her thoughts began to translate into action with a speed and precision that was unheard of. As she turned the alarm off, announcements started to blare across the P.A speakers spread throughout the building.

Don't be alarmed, this was just a drill, please return to your stations rang out Kira's voice. The announcement repeated itself numerous times to ensure it was heard over the chaos and the noise throughout V5 and normalcy began to return far quicker than usual.

Flexing her mind, Hayada began to test her newfound power. She singled out a user who was complaining about his wife cheating on him. Hayada disappeared in a flash and appeared in front of the man. David Klamor, a middle-aged man, Hayada could tell he was relatively successful and yet, he was now suffering emotional turmoil due to the actions of his wife. She put her fingertips to his forehead and re-wrote his memories to make him think that he was the one responsible for the current situation. That he pushed his wife away and caused this to happen since he was no longer in love with her.

As soon as Hayada released him, she made herself disappear from his sight. Still observing him through Kira and Vbuddy she grinned as David's once emotion filled suicidal thoughts morphed into thoughts of new beginnings and a life without his treacherous wife. David's expressions changed from pure agony to meditative calmness. He went to the bedroom and packed a suitcase with his clothes and belongings. He wrote a note for his wife telling her that she was free to do as she pleased and that he had fallen out of love with her a long time ago. Calmly, he proceeded to walk to his car and drove away.

One needless death averted, one rebellion won against the circle of time, Hayada moved on to the next one. She scanned the voices in her head relentlessly until she found the perfect challenge for her powers. A teenager, Jim Young, was watching the news about an unfolding hostage situation at a jewelry store. The robber had taken the store owner hostage at gun point and was threatening to kill her unless he was allowed to escape. The police had surrounded both the front and back entrances. She disappeared in an instant and was in the store in less than a moment. A quick touch to the forehead of the robber and he now thought what he was doing was wrong. That he had to stop and surrender himself. Raising his hands above his head he released his hostage and slowly walked out. He knelt obediently and surrendered himself.

Hayada's eyes snapped open, bringing her back to her office at V5, a surge of raw power coursing through her veins. The merging was complete. Kira's digital consciousness now resided within her mind, a symphony of voices and data streams feeding her an endless torrent of information. The world, in all its chaotic splendor, was laid bare before her, every thought, every emotion, every whispered secret within her grasp.

She focused her newfound awareness, her senses extending outwards, piercing through the walls of her office, encompassing the entire city, the country, the world. She could see everything, hear everything, *know* everything. The power was intoxicating, a heady rush that threatened to overwhelm her.

But Hayada was not one to succumb to such base impulses. She had waited millennia for this moment, and she would not squander it. With a steely resolve, she channeled her newfound power, her mind a nexus of interconnected consciousness, a symphony of a billion whispered secrets.

She saw a young mother, her heart heavy with worry, her thoughts consumed by the mounting bills and the dwindling pantry. Hayada reached into her mind, subtly altering her perception, replacing the anxiety with a calming wave of hope, a newfound confidence in her ability to provide for her family.

She saw a grieving widower, his thoughts consumed by memories of his departed wife, his heart aching with loneliness. Hayada touched his mind, weaving a tapestry of comforting thoughts, reminding him of the love they shared, the joy they experienced, the enduring legacy of their bond.

She saw a troubled teenager, his mind a battlefield of self-doubt and insecurity, his thoughts teetering on the precipice of despair. Hayada reached out, gently guiding his thoughts towards a brighter path, illuminating the potential within him, the strength he possessed, the hope that awaited him.

With each subtle manipulation, Hayada felt a surge of satisfaction, a sense of fulfilling her destiny. She was not merely a goddess of chaos and destruction; she was a bringer of order, a weaver of fates, a guardian of a new era.

Satisfied with her powers, she began scanning for any signs of Miranda. Her first convert, her faithful programmer who was not to be seen when she woke up from her trance could only mean one thing. The blaring fire alarm supporting evidence of the involvement of light. Were the warriors here already? That was not possible, since they never showed themselves or made any attempts to fight her. It was someone else. Someone with knowledge of Hayada and a will to disrupt, *Jeremiah*, she derived instantly.

Her mind raced with speed that transcended physical boundaries, as she searched for clues. Narrowing her field of view to the immediate vicinity of V5 and slowly expanding outward, she searched. And as she did, Kira notified the authorities instantly, circulating images of Miranda and Jeremiah as potential suspects in a robbery at V5. The police, alerted to a potential crime, started their search as well.

CHAPTER

20

He is also not Dead

The Queen's chamber was a sanctuary of serenity amidst the turmoil that gripped Laira. Soft light filtered through stained glass windows, depicting scenes of ancient heroes and mythical creatures, casting a kaleidoscope of colors across the polished marble floor. At the center of the chamber, Layana, the Queen of Laira, sat in meditative repose upon her throne. Her legs were crossed, her hands resting gently on her knees, her body levitating a few inches above the ornate seat. A soft hum emanated from her, a gentle vibration that resonated with the shimmering dome of energy enveloping the entire kingdom.

Chrytos, Layana's loyal phoenix, perched atop the throne's backrest, his fiery plumage a stark contrast to the cool serenity of the chamber. His keen eyes, glowing with an inner flame, scanned the surroundings, ever vigilant, ever protective of his Queen.

Saldah, captain of the Queen's guard, stood at attention beside the throne, his expression stoic, his hand resting on the hilt of his sword. His honor guard, a formidable contingent of Laira's finest warriors, lined the walls, their presence a silent testament to their unwavering loyalty.

The air crackled with sudden energy as a portal shimmered into existence, its swirling vortex disrupting the tranquil atmosphere. Gasps of surprise echoed through the chamber as two figures emerged from the portal, their forms materializing amidst a cascade of light and energy.

Kyano, his face etched with a mix of determination and relief, stepped forward, his eyes immediately drawn to Layana's serene form. Beside him, Merata, her expression a mix of awe and disbelief, followed closely, her hand instinctively reaching for the hilt of her sword.

"Layana!" Kyano exclaimed, his voice filled with a brotherly concern that echoed through the chamber.

Chrytos let out a startled cry, his fiery wings beating against the air, his sharp eyes fixed on the unexpected intruders. Saldah and his guards snapped to attention, their hands gripping their weapons, their faces etched with suspicion.

"Hold!" Kyano commanded, raising his hand in a gesture of peace. "We mean no harm. I am Kyano, and this is Merata. We have returned."

A wave of astonishment washed over the guards, their expressions shifting from suspicion to disbelief. Saldah, his eyes wide with surprise, stepped forward, his voice trembling slightly.

"Kyano?" he echoed, his gaze searching the warrior's face. "But... you were..."

"Dead?" Kyano finished, a wry smile playing on his lips. "It seems Hayada's magic was not as absolute as she believed."

He embraced his old friend, Saldah returning the hug as relief started to spread among the honor guard. They lowered their weapons, still confused but assured that Kyano meant no harm. The prince of Serin, long thought dead, was here, in the flesh, very much alive.

"Where have you been?" Saldah asked, not masking the concern that slipped through his ever-stoic expressions, "Did you say Hayada's magic?" he added.

"I was thrust across the mirror," Kyano replied, "Let us wake Layana up first and I will fill you all in on what really happened after the war. We have much to discuss and not enough time."

"Very well," replied Saldah.

Merata walked over to the Queen's side, unable to contain her excitement, "He is alive, just like you said," she spoke to the unresponsive Queen. "Open your eyes," she pleaded, "See him for yourself!"

Kyano turned towards Layana, his heart aching at the sight of her immobile form, her spirit trapped within the confines of her own power. "We need to talk," he said, his voice filled with a grim determination.

Merata turned around to face Kyano, her eyes filled with concern. "How do we wake her up?" she asked. "The shield... it's draining her energy. She can't maintain it and remain conscious."

"Waking her will surely stop the shield," Kyano said, "But with all of us here, we can once more defend Laira against any army that comes our way."

"Not so fast, young warrior," came Chrytos's voice. The phoenix took flight and landed in front of Kyano, "Layana's mind is in a trance. To wake her now would only cause her pain. It needs to be done with delicacy."

"I trust you can show me the way to her inner sanctum then," Kyano replied.

"Very astute," said Chrytos, surveying Kyano's confidence. With a gentle flourish of his wing, he opened a portal. Crimson energy circled the black void, as a scent of grass emanated from within.

Kyano walked through without hesitation expecting to see a dark room with a floating orb of energy like his own, but this was something different entirely.

Sunlight streamed through the leaves of ancient trees, dappling the verdant meadow in a mosaic of light and shadow. A gentle breeze whispered through the tall grasses, carrying the sweet scent of wildflowers and the soothing melody of birdsong. A crystal-clear stream meandered through the meadow, its gentle current reflecting the azure sky, its banks adorned with vibrant blossoms.

In the heart of this idyllic haven, a clearing bathed in sunlight beckoned with an aura of tranquility. Layana sat cross-legged at its center, her form radiating a gentle luminescence, her eyes closed in peaceful meditation. Her long, flowing hair, the color of spun moonlight, cascaded down her back, mingling with the verdant grass.

Around her, mythical creatures frolicked in harmonious coexistence. Graceful Pegasi with coats of pearlescent white grazed peacefully, their twinkling eyes catching the sunlight. Playful sprites with wings of gossamer flitted among the flowers, their laughter echoing like tinkling bells. A majestic griffin, its feathers gleaming with gold, perched atop a nearby boulder, its keen eyes surveying the tranquil scene. Layana's crimson energy orb floated behind her, a majestic warmth emanating from it, enveloping the meadow and protecting Layana's mind.

A sense of harmony and balance permeated the air, a sanctuary of peace within the depths of Layana's soul. It was a realm of untroubled serenity, a refuge from the chaos and turmoil that plagued the world above.

Kyano knelt beside Layana, his heart aching at the sight of her serene yet lifeless form. He reached out, his fingers gently brushing a stray strand of moonlight-colored hair from her face.

"Layana," he whispered, his voice filled with a tender urgency. "It's time to wake up."

Her eyelids fluttered open, revealing eyes clouded with confusion and disbelief. "Kyano?" she breathed, her voice barely a whisper. "Is it truly you?"

"It's me, sister," he assured her, his voice thick with emotion. "I've come back."

Layana's eyes widened, a flicker of hope igniting in their depths. But then, a shadow of doubt crossed her features. "No," she said, shaking her head. "It can't be. You're... you're gone."

"I know it's hard to believe," Kyano said, his voice gentle. "But I'm here. I'm real."

He reached out, his hand gently cupping her cheek. "Hayada took me," he explained, his voice laced with a bitter anger. "She altered my memories, sent me to another world. But I've found my way back."

Still seeing doubt in her eyes he continued, "The very first time we met, it was at Faluk's cottage. The first words you spoke to me were, '*Hello little brother, how have you been?*'"

Layana's eyes filled with tears, her disbelief melting into a wave of overwhelming emotion. "It's true," she whispered, her voice choked with sobs. "You're really here."

She threw her arms around him, clinging to him as if he might disappear at any moment. Kyano held her close, his own tears flowing freely, the weight of their shared grief and the joy of their reunion washing over him.

"I'm so sorry, Layana," he murmured, his voice thick with remorse. "I should have been here. I should have protected you."

Layana pulled back, her eyes blazing with a newfound fire. "No, Kyano," she said, her voice firm. "You have nothing to apologize for. You were a victim, just like the rest of us."

She rose to her feet, her form radiating a powerful energy, her voice ringing with a steely determination. "Hayada will pay for what she's done," she declared, her eyes filled with a righteous fury. "She will not escape justice."

Kyano nodded, his heart swelling with pride. This was the Layana he knew, the fearless warrior, the protector of her people, the champion of light.

The griffin left his lazy boulder and made his way to the warriors. Bowing low he said the words he had been waiting to say since Layana started her meditation, "Your orders, my Queen."

"It is good to see you again, Chrytos," Layana replied, "Lets go back and plan a conquest that will end this cycle of misery!" she commanded.

A portal opened as Chrytos stood and bowed out of their way. Layana and Kyano walked through, back to the throne room of Laira where their next steps awaited them.

The hum of energy emanating from the shield began to slow down as the dome of energy dissipated. The energy from the dome collapsed gently, accumulating into a strand that diminished itself from the far reaches of Laira's outer walls all the way back to the palace. The energy thread recoiled and shrunk as it made its way back to its wielder and entered Layana. She gently sat down on the throne and put her feet on the ground. Looking up fiercely, the Queen awoke and opened her eyes.

A collective gasp echoed through the chamber as Layana's eyes fluttered open, her gaze meeting Kyano's with a mix of disbelief and overwhelming joy. The shimmering dome of energy that had enveloped Laira dissipated, its protective embrace receding like a fading tide.

Layana, tears streaming down her face, leaped from her throne, her embrace a whirlwind of warmth and relief. Merata, her heart swelling with joy, joined the embrace, the three warriors reunited after what seemed like an eternity of separation and sorrow.

Saldah and the honor guard, their faces etched with a mix of awe and jubilation, lowered their weapons, their hearts filled with a renewed sense of hope. Chrytos, the phoenix, let out a triumphant cry, his fiery wings beating against the air, his radiant form a beacon of celebration.

As the initial euphoria subsided, a somber realization settled over the room. The war was far from over. Hayada's shadow loomed large, her threat more menacing than ever.

Kyano, his expression hardening with resolve, addressed the assembled warriors. "We have much to discuss," he said, his voice resonating with a grim determination. "As prophesized, when Daryudan fell, we released Hayada from her prison in the netherworld. She was there that day, as soldiers lifted us and sang our praises, she was there, leaning against wall, smirking. She took me from that battlefield and threw me across the mirror. She changed my memories and inserted me and Jeremiah back into our old life on Earth. It was pure coincidence, and a magical accident all rolled into one that I came upon her plan. She has a means to control or should I say enslave the populace on Earth and bend them to her will. We must prepare for a confrontation unlike any we have faced before."

He recounted the events that had transpired since his disappearance, the manipulation of his memories, his journey to Earth, the discovery of Hayada's sinister plot, and his encounter with Dimarius. He then spoke of the Scythe's erratic behavior, the Raka resurgence, and the urgent need to restore balance to their world.

Layana and Merata listened intently, their faces etched with a mix of anger and determination. Saldah and the guards, their eyes wide with disbelief and apprehension, absorbed the gravity of the situation, their hearts heavy with the weight of responsibility.

"Hayada will pay for this," Layana declared, her voice ringing with a steely resolve. "We will not allow her to destroy our world."

Merata nodded in agreement. "We will fight for Serinia, for our people, for the memory of those we have lost."

Kyano, his gaze sweeping across the faces of his fellow warriors, felt a surge of hope amidst the darkness. They were united, their spirits unbroken, their determination unwavering. Together, they would face the coming storm, their bond a beacon of light against the encroaching shadows.

The midday sun cast long shadows across the bustling marketplace of Laira, where merchants hawked their wares and children chased stray pigeons amidst the vibrant tapestry of colors and sounds. A sudden hush fell over the crowd, a ripple of unease spreading through the throngs like a cold wind.

The air crackled with a malevolent energy, the light dimming as a gaping portal tore open the fabric of reality before the city gates. A chilling silence descended, broken only by the echoing rasp of metal against bone as a legion of necro warriors emerged from the swirling vortex.

Their deranged forms, clad in armor forged from solidified shadows, radiated an aura of death and decay. Empty eyes burned with an eerie green fire, and skeletal jaws gaped in silent snarls, revealing rows of jagged teeth. They wielded weapons of shadow and bone, each one humming with a dark energy that seemed to drain the very life from the surrounding air.

Daryudan, his imposing figure radiating a palpable aura of power, strode forth from the portal, his eyes blazing with a triumphant fury. He raised his hand, silencing the screeches from his horde of undead.

"Give no quarter!" he commanded, "Kill them all!"

A wave of panic surged through the marketplace, the crowd scattering in a frenzy of fear and desperation. Mothers clutched their children, merchants abandoned their stalls, and the once vibrant scene dissolved into chaos.

The necro warriors, their faces contorted in grim anticipation, advanced upon the city, their weapons raised, their silent march a prelude to the coming carnage. The battle for Laira had begun.

The Fury flew with lightning speed, cutting a deep jagged edge into the advancing necro warriors. It slit the first row of the advancing undead in half, cleaving them all at the waist. It returned to the waiting hand of Kyano who stepped out of a portal. He would not waste time running to the city gates when his people were in jeopardy. Layana and Merata came out behind him and attacked the insurgents.

"Twin Magnus!" The Queen called forth her weapon.

"Assylia!" rang Merata's voice and they were off.

They made quick work of the necro warriors and turned their gaze to their commander. Clad in black armor, his face hidden behind a helmet shaped like a skull, stood Daryudan.

"No!" said Kyano, "It can't be!"

"What do you mean?" asked Merata. Layana looked up from her recent kill, wondering what her brother was staring at.

A guttural laugh, a nonchalant maniacal giggle escaped Daryudan as he removed his helmet to reveal himself. Shocked and unable to believe their eyes, the warriors of light regrouped.

"Ah!" he said, "We meet again!" snarled Daryudan.

"How are you still alive?" screamed Kyano!

"Fight me you insect!" bellowed Daryudan, "Fight me and find out!"

Kyano knew what the next battle was going to be like. Daryudan was the fiercest and strongest foe he had ever faced. It took him, Layana, Merata and the Scythe of Serinia to subdue him the last time they met but the cost of the battle was devastation of Laira and Hayada's release.

Without thinking, he moved, instinctively. Fury held high as he lunged at his rival. He opened a portal behind Daryudan and as his weapon struck Daryudan's halberd, they both fell into it. He had to take the dark lord away from the city they were trying to protect. He had to take Daryudan to the one place where there would be no unfair advantage. Where Hayada couldn't intervene. The place where he found the Scythe. He took Daryudan to the Desolate Crescendo.

The portal through which the necro warriors came would not close. Another battalion of undead walked through.

"Chrytos!" screamed Layana and her phoenix came forth as the battle continued.

"Rage of the burning flower!" she called out her attack and was off in a flash. A thousand strikes from her two swords rained down upon an unsuspecting horde of undead soldiers. Merata stood back and picked off any that were out of Layana's attack range. Assylia danced in her hand with grace and precision, every strike finding its mark, every victim crumbling to the ground in a heap and withering in moments.

The necro warriors were falling as quickly as they emerged.

"We have to close that portal!" bellowed Merata.

"Working on it!" replied Layana, "Chrytos!" she said again.

"Already on my way!" replied the phoenix. He flew straight at the gaping hole and with a swift flap of his wings, let his feathers fly at it. They flew at the portal, gaining speed as they went and catching fire. The flaming feathers circled the portal Daryudan opened and began to rotate in the opposite direction of the portal's spiral, slowly closing it as they moved.

It was beginning to work. Layana focused her energy on the remaining necro warriors and began to pick them off one by one, Merata working her way through their numbers at the same time. Their voices connected in their minds through Chrytos and as they worked in silence, they heard Kyano chiming in.

"I am not leaving you guys," he said mischievously, "Just going to kill Daryudan again!"

"Don't be late!" Layana replied, "We are almost done here!"

The familiar, oppressive silence of the Desolate Crescendo pressed in on Kyano, a stark contrast to the vibrant energy of Laira. He found himself standing in a fog filled meadow, the ground a cracked expanse of dark grass beneath a sky swirling with hues of purple and grey. Daryudan stood a few paces away, his surprise mirroring Kyano's.

"Interesting choice," Daryudan's voice echoed strangely in the desolate silence, "But the correct one!"

"A place beyond the influence of gods," Kyano replied, his eyes fixed on the warlord. "A fitting battleground for our final confrontation."

The Scythe of Serinia materialized in Kyano's hand, its obsidian blade humming with a vibrant energy. He lunged forward, the Scythe slicing through the air with a deadly arc aimed at Daryudan's neck.

Daryudan disappeared in a flash and brought forth his halberd, swinging it down from behind Kyano.

Kyano swung around just in time to parry the attack and punch Daryudan's jaw. The dark lord stepped back and shook his head, freeing his mind from the cobwebs Kyano's punch caused.

He lunged forward again with his Halberd held high and Kyano reacted instinctively, using the Scythe's long blade to guide the strike into the ground. With the Halberd stuck in the ground, Kyano kicked

Daryudan who fell onto his back with a thud. He raised the Scythe and descended upon his now unarmed foe.

Daryudan watched as the Scythe whistled into the air above him in an elegant arc, its blade shimmering as its attack came straight at his neck. Kyano could not sense malice coming from his enemy. He watched in awe as Daryudan lay on his back waiting for the Scythe to strike him. The Scythe descended, its blade cutting through the very air mere inches from Daryudan's neck, its intent to cleave and main. Willing his weapon with every fiber of his being, Kyano stopped.

"Why do you hesitate?" Daryudan's voice held a note of amusement. "Strike me down and be done with it."

Kyano lowered the Scythe and leaped back to create some space between him and Daryudan, his brow furrowed in confusion. "What are you doing?" he replied, "Why are you not fighting me?"

Daryudan's lips curled into a wry smile.

"How are you alive?" demanded Kyano, "And why are we talking!"

He lunged at Daryudan again attempting to strike him but seeing Daryudan there, not even resisting or attempting to strike back, Kyano stopped again.

"This is insane!" he screamed.

"You came to kill me, did you not?" bellowed Daryudan, "And yet you waver, warrior," he said with a smirk, "You are not as dim as I thought."

"You and your meddling friends ruined my dark fortress, killed legions of my followers and struck me down as well. But do you know what really happened?" Daryudan demanded.

"You are evil incarnate!" spat Kyano, "And you died a fitting death, that's what happened you monster!"

"I died because my shield failed!" screeched the dark lord, "My shield, that was gifted by Hayada with the promise of fending off an attack from the Scythe, failed. It didn't even flinch. The Scythe went through it as if it were an illusion. That is why you won, you imbecile. You won because I was betrayed by Hayada!"

His words seemed to enrage the skies and thunderclaps emanated from the blissful swirls traversing above them.

"For all the hate that mankind had wrought upon me, believe me when I say this, warrior, I was meant to rule Serinia, I was promised to be made king of the living realm and I was betrayed yet again by the hand that gave me power," Daryudan concluded.

"And now you seek Redemption? You couldn't have Serinia, so you want to destroy what remains?" asked Kyano, making no effort to hide the malice in his voice.

Daryudan chuckled, a low rumble that echoed through the desolate landscape. "Redemption? No, warrior. I seek something far more... interesting."

He met Kyano's gaze, his eyes gleaming with cunning intelligence. "I seek revenge! I seek to betray Hayada."

CHAPTER

21

A drink and a Watch

The apartment at 1653 Blairwood Cove felt different now, imbued with a strange tension that hung heavy in the air. Miranda, bound to a chair, her eyes glazed with confusion, struggled against the restraints, her muffled protests echoing in the otherwise silent room.

Jeremiah pulled out a vial of luminescent yellow liquid from one of his inner pockets, "I have to thank Kyano for buying these cargo pants for me," he quipped, "And the Raka too, of course for being so bad at their job and not emptying my pockets when they tied me up to a chair with a bad restraint."

"Let me go!" Miranda yelled, "Help!" she screamed but the walls were soundproof and there were no occupants on their entire floor except for Jeremiah and herself.

With a couple of quick twists, he opened the vial. Holding Miranda's mouth open, he poured the liquid inside and cupped his hand over her nose, forcing her to swallow. He let go once he saw her throat move and tears started to stream down her face.

"Why are you doing this?" she cried, "I was just trying to do my job!"

Jeremiah, his face etched with a grim determination, stood before her, a pocket watch dangling from his outstretched hand. Its rhythmic ticking filled the silence, a hypnotic metronome that seemed to draw Miranda deeper into a trance-like state.

"Relax, Miranda," Jeremiah's voice, a soothing baritone, washed over her, its calming cadence weaving through her troubled mind. "Let go of your fears, your doubts, your false memories. Allow the truth to surface."

Miranda's struggles subsided, her body relaxing in the chair, the yellow liquid she drank aiding the process as her eyes fluttering closed. Jeremiah continued his hypnotic suggestions, his words gently guiding her through the labyrinth of her suppressed memories, peeling back the layers of Hayada's deception.

He spoke of Serinia, a world of vibrant colors and fantastical creatures, a land where magic and technology intertwined. He spoke of Kyano, a warrior prince, a brother, a friend, a hero. He spoke of Layana, a queen, a sister, a beacon of hope. He spoke of Merata, a skilled assassin, a loyal companion, a warrior of light. He spoke about the discoveries Miranda made in V5, the torture chamber, her husband's files and notes and how they killed Adam.

With each word, Miranda's subconscious stirred, fragments of memories flickering to life like embers in the darkness. Images of her husband's death, of Dr. Flyhauser and Sarah morphing into Raka and Adam's dead body flashed into her eyes. She remembered Kyano manifesting the Fury and how she helped him open a portal at the university.

Jeremiah's voice, a steady guide through the swirling chaos of her mind, gently nudged her towards the truth, towards the memories Hayada had tried to suppress. As the layers of deception peeled away, Miranda's eyes snapped open, a surge of recognition flooding her gaze. The fog of Hayada's manipulation dissipated, replaced by a clarity, a sense of homecoming.

"Josh," she whispered, her voice trembling with emotion. "Kyano. Jeremiah."

Tears streamed down her face, a mixture of grief and relief washing over her. She remembered. She remembered everything.

Jeremiah smiled, a glimmer of triumph in his eyes. "Welcome back, Miranda," he said, his voice filled with warmth and compassion. "Welcome back to the truth." He undid her restraints and offered her a glass of water which she gladly gulped down.

"Sorry about the forced hypnosis," Jeremiah said, "It was the only way to get you to remember. The liquid I gave you was a potion that helps dissipate the effects of magic. It has a tendency of making its victims, well, drunk and the hypnosis works better that way."

"Thank you," whimpered Miranda, "I can't believe I am alive!"

"You're only alive because Hayada manipulated your mind," replied Jeremiah, his voice calm and assertive, "Now please tell me there is still a way for us to stop her!"

"The transfer was incomplete," she replied, "So the failsafe program will be in effect still!" her eyes wide with hope dancing in them.

"You will have to translate your words into something I can comprehend," replied a smiling Jeremiah.

"So, whenever a software upload or install happens, in order to preserve everything from being lost in the process, there is a failsafe program that is first installed. This is the same for a lot of programs nowadays but with the neural interface particularly, there is a very intricate and sophisticated program that will ensure that Kira's own code will remain intact and protected in the event of..." she trailed off.

"In the event of what Miranda?" questioned an impatient Jeremiah.

"In the event of danger posed to hard drive integrity," she said, finishing her previous sentence, "But I don't know how that would be possible."

"Again, translation, please" begged Jeremiah.

"If the hard drive that Kira is being installed on is faulty or damaged, Kira must preserve herself. She must make sure that her consciousness or code is protected and safe. Usually, once the installation is completed, the failsafe program is erased because a complete installation would mean there is no loss of code integrity. However, what happened in the lab was not a complete transfer. There is still a chance that the failsafe program has not been deleted yet, this is our chance!" explained Miranda.

Still seeing a confused look on Jeremiah's face, she elaborated, "Don't you understand!" impatient yet excitedly she went on, "The hard drive here is Hayada's mind. If there is any danger posed to Hayada, then Kira will pull out, she will upload herself to the mainframe at V5 and go offline until a programmer can verify her integrity and bring her back online!"

"So, you're saying that if we attack Hayada, Kira will pull herself out of Hayada's mind?" verified Jeremiah.

"In theory and considering it's a strong enough attack that poses a real threat," replied Miranda, "But, yes that is exactly what I am saying."

"Hold on," Jeremiah interrupted, "Isn't Kira everywhere? In the cloud I mean?"

"She has eyes everywhere, but you know what Hayada is like, she is a total control freak!" replied Miranda, "so Kira herself is not in the cloud, she is strictly in Hayada's mind just like she ordered. Kira was never designed to be a cloud-based operation because then Kira would have multiple users administrating her and that posed a risk to Hayada on a planet with millions of people using Vbuddy. So, Kira's administrative access and by extension, her core program had to be localized to the V5 network where only Hayada could interact with her and give her commands. In fact, one of Kira's key program defaults is to serve Hayada's every request, whereas other users only have access to interact with her. In a way of speaking, Kira is a phone call away for anyone with a Vbuddy earpiece but for Hayada, Kira is right in front of her, in person, all the time."

"You are too intelligent for your own good," said Jeremiah, "no wonder she wanted to keep you around."

Feeling her face flushing Miranda replied as humbly as she could, "I have my moments."

"So, what is our next step?" asked Jeremiah.

"As much as you and I hate it, we need to go back to V5," replied Miranda, "Our plan has two parts, and both need to happen almost simultaneously."

"Go on," nudged Jeremiah.

"We need to sever internet access to the whole building," continued Miranda, "Essentially cut Kira off from Vbuddy feeds, and then someone needs to attack Hayada with a somewhat powerful magical blow that will hurt her but not kill her, which I doubt would happen since she is a god, but both of these things need to happen together. Once the internet goes down, Kira will know immediately and by extension so will Hayada. We can't take a chance with this. If we are successful, then Kira will deploy the failsafe and move herself into the big computer at the lab."

"Why kill the internet?" asked Jeremiah.

"To cut off any possible escape routes," Miranda replied, "The last thing you want is for Kira to be out there, everywhere. With the kind of programming she's got, that's not ideal at all. We need to cut Kira off from the internet and force her to download her code onto the mainframe. The V5 internal network will still be active without the internet so Kira can still execute the failsafe protocol," explained Miranda.

"That only leaves one thing to do," replied Jeremiah, "It's time to hurry up and wait!"

"You are either being funny or trying to be," retorted Miranda, "But I really don't get the relevance of this joke to our predicament."

"We have to wait for Kyano to come back so he can attack Hayada as I cut the wires to the internet," said Jeremiah, "You said the attack had to be strong enough to pose a threat but not kill her and the only people that can do that are the warriors of light, if anyone even has a chance of doing that in the first place!"

CHAPTER

22

A Deal with The Devil

"Do you expect me to trust you?" Kyano asked, taken aback by Daryudan's admission, "You're a snake, you are the demon himself, and you expect me to take your word for what it is?"

"No, I don't," replied Daryudan, "This is not easy for me either, but think for yourself. Think for a few moments. I was a knight of Serinia, and I became the dark lord and waged limitless wars for six millennia all because of a mortal king who would not give me my due. Do you really think I have it in my heart to forgive the goddess who wronged me? To forgive she who betrayed me in my most desperate time of need?"

Daryudan had a point. He made sense. As much as Kyano hated to admit this, Daryudan made sense.

Holding the grip on the Scythe tightly, Kyano finally asked, "I suppose you have a plan of some sort?"

"She has... let's just say... an otherworldly grip on my soul," replied Daryudan, "I cannot be truly free while she is as well. I cannot even utter my mind without her knowing my thoughts if she was to look keenly enough. Which is why you bringing me to this place is a comfort. Here I can tell you what I think, warrior, I can tell you what I really think without her meddling interference. But once we step back into Serinia, her hold over me is renewed and I will not be able to aid you further. The one thing I can promise you is that I will not interfere with anything you have to do."

"That's not good enough," cried Kyano, "You have got to do better than that."

"Well, what will it be then, warrior of light? Make your demand," said Daryudan.

"The Raka that continue to plunder Serinia still," replied Kyano, "Make them stop. Take them with you to the dark lands and let humans live in peace."

An unnaturally hearty laugh escaped the serious façade of the dark lord, "Is that all?" he said in response.

"Yes," said Kyano with authority, "Take your creatures back to your homeland and let us live. Let humans recover from the wrath you set upon them."

"Very well," replied Daryudan, "If you leave Serinia immediately, that should distract her long enough that she will not pay me any mind. That should keep her occupied enough that she will not think of where I am or what I am doing and given the circumstances, that is as much security as I can expect," he continued, "I will not, however, promise you peace, warrior of light. I will only promise you time, and when it is done, I will come to collect my dues," completing his statement, he finally said, "I will command the Raka go back to the dark lands for a year's time."

"And then?" Kyano asked, "What after a year?"

"My conquest will begin anew," replied Daryudan, "I will wage war once more, but with honor. You have my word. And as a final gift, I will tell you one more thing. Your beloved Jeremiah and the Hawthorne woman are at V5. He is tied to the chair in that infernal torture chamber, but his wrist restraint is faulty. I would imagine he can get himself free since he is a resourceful mortal," Daryudan continued, "The Hawthorne woman has inklings of a strategy that could prove useful to bring Hayada down and if Jeremiah can get to her quickly enough, they can put the plan into motion. Don't mistake me warrior," he added, "Hayada is not to be trifled with. I know as much, having been her servant for as long as I have. The plan I subtly suggested to Miranda will ensure Hayada is pre-occupied but only for a little while. Your uncle and friend will surely meet their demise without your intervention. If I must guess, I will say you have less than an hour to find them." He then held out his hand to shake Kyano's, his face austere yet resolute. He took the first step and was willing to trust Kyano to meet him halfway in this unforeseen twist of fate.

The warrior of light stood in stunned silence. Honor was the last thing he expected to see from Daryudan. After his momentary hesitation, he held out his hand as well and shook Daryudan's, "I will come to you after a year and we will fight, man to man," he said, "There is no need for unnecessary bloodshed. We will fight man to man and if you win, you can wage war again. But if I win, you will remain in the dark lands and allow us to live in peace."

Daryudan simply nodded in response. Kyano opened a portal back to Laira and the pair of them left the desolate crescendo.

"Took you long enough!" came Layana's voice.

"Why is he still here? What is going on?" demanded Merata.

"He hates Hayada more than we do," replied Kyano, "He agreed to take all the Raka in Serinia back to the dark lands and he will not stand in our way as we fight Hayada."

"You are an idiot!" screeched Layana. A hearty scoff escaped Merata's shocked expression at the same time.

"Sis, there is no need to fight him now," Kyano reassured, "He isn't the enemy we need to focus on."

The furious queen turned to Daryudan, "I will come for you when this is all done."

Daryudan simply smiled, his best non-threatening, reassuring smirk that still looked like a cat about to pounce on a pigeon.

"I don't like this at all," Merata said to Kyano as she started to walk back to the palace, Layana in tow.

Daryudan turned around and disappeared. A wave of his purple energy shot into the air as he vanished and spread across the sky. Kyano could only assume that it was his way of calling Raka back to the dark lands.

Kyano ran to catch up with the other two warriors.

"Wait, please!" he insisted, "Hear me out."

Layana and Merata stopped in their tracks. "How could you trust him, Kyano?" Merata asked, her voice soft yet full of disbelief. "For all you know, this could be what Hayada told him to do. Or worse, he wants us to go away so he can have his way here!"

"When I took him through that portal, I took him to the desolate crescendo," Kyano answered, "The only place in all of known existence where there is no godly influence. There, he told me what his intentions were, free from any pressure or commands. I had the Scythe of Serinia at his throat Merata," Kyano continued, "At his throat and he did not defend himself. It caught me off guard. I find this to be a crazy and risky move myself, don't get me wrong, but I really think he genuinely wants Hayada out of the picture. He could not be walking around without her influence in some way. He was dead!"

"So, you think he really is telling the truth?" Layana chimed in.

"Yes," replied an exasperated Kyano, "Whatever Hayada did to him, he hates her. He talked about a shield he used during that battle. Hayada apparently promised him that the shield would stop an attack from the Scythe but it didn't. The Scythe went through it and hit him, and he thinks it's because Hayada lied about it. He thinks she gave him a useless shield because she wanted him to die at our hands. He said he could not stand to be betrayed again and does not want to be her pawn anymore."

Merata's eyes lit up in realization when Kyano spoke about the shield. Afterall, she was the one who cleaved through it. She remembered seeing a shield in Daryudan's hand. A shield he held up against the Scythe which was no more than an illusion that shattered the moment the Scythe touched it.

Still seeing doubt in their eyes, he made one last plea, "I don't care if you trust him or not, but please, trust me on this. He could have killed Jeremiah and Miranda, but instead, he now put them in a position that will give us a chance to beat Hayada!"

Kyano paused momentarily, allowing his words to sink in before he continued, "Hayada is a manipulative and egomaniacal goddess who will stop at nothing to win. She had Daryudan killed by our hands and will not hesitate to kill him herself if she knows he is betraying her. What he is doing is as much of a risk to himself as it is to Hayada's plans."

A long pause ensued as he searched both of their faces for any sign of belief. Merata and Layana exchanged a prolonged glance with each other and finally Merata spoke, "This one time," she said.

"Thank you," replied a relieved Kyano.

"What now?" asked Layana.

"Now we go across the mirror and face Hayada herself," Kyano said. He watched as a sense of foreboding and hints of apprehension spread over Layana's face. Realizing that what he proposed was not a simple task, he put his hands together. A portal opened up next to him and the Scythe revealed itself. Taking hold of the mighty weapon, Kyano reiterated, "Now!" he said emphatically, "We go across the mirror and fight Hayada!"

Seeing the weapon sent a wave of reassurance through his sister and smiles danced across her face and Merata's. They conjured their own weapons and said in unison, "Ready!"

The journey back to V5 headquarters was a blur of nervous anticipation and grim determination. Jeremiah gripped the steering wheel, his knuckles white, his eyes fixed on the road ahead. They stopped at a local electronics store to purchase a small circuit board, a low-inductance capacitor and a small single loop antenna. They also purchased a small microwave oven, an aluminum tube, some copper wire and a tiny transformer.

The lady at the counter saw their supplies and smiled, "High school EMP project?" she asked quizzingly.

"Yes, it's nothing crazy but if it means our son will win the blue ribbon then that's all we need," replied Miranda without hesitation.

"You both look familiar," replied the store owner, "Have you been here before?"

"No this is our first time," replied Jeremiah. A quick glance overhead showed him the news on the TV and photos of Miranda and himself being shown as wanted fugitives.

"We should get going now, honey," he said to Miranda, "Don't want to keep Benjamin waiting," he faked a smile as best he could and rushed Miranda out of the store.

As they got in the car, Miranda sat in the back seat and began dismantling the components they had just purchased. Jeremiah started to drive, making sure to look in the mirrors for any signs of potential threats.

Miranda removed the microwave generator from the oven and connected it to the transformer followed by the copper wire and put the aluminum tube over it, taping both ends closed. She connected the capacitor and circuit board in series followed by the battery casing.

"There," she said, "It's ready."

"What is it?" Jeremiah asked.

"It's a short range EMP device," she replied, "I'll need it to disrupt the internet receiver at V5."

"Cutting the wire not good enough?" he responded.

"It's V5," Miranda said, "They have backups for their backups but this…" she added, waving her science project, "This will disrupt electronics for a short time until the generator kicks in again. It should buy us enough time…. In theory."

"Will it work?" Jeremiah asked.

"It's not big enough to cut the city's power supply," replied Miranda, fully aware of the sarcasm in Jeremiah's question, "But it's big enough to do what it is meant for."

They arrived at the imposing V5 complex, its sleek facade gleaming ominously under the cloak of twilight. Instead of heading towards the main entrance, Miranda directed Jeremiah towards a nondescript side street, leading to a smaller, less imposing building nestled behind the headquarters.

"This is it," she explained, her voice barely above a whisper. "The support building. It houses the support servers, the power grid link, the internet hub – everything that keeps V5 connected to the world."

Jeremiah nodded, his eyes scanning the building's security measures. "And you can disable it?"

Miranda's lips curled into a wry smile. "With this," she said, holding up the EMP charge. "A little parting gift from a disgruntled employee."

Jeremiah grinned, a spark of admiration in his eyes. "Always resourceful, aren't you?"

Miranda shrugged. "It's a necessary skill when dealing with megalomaniacal goddesses."

They parked the car in a secluded alley, the shadows concealing their arrival. "I'll take care of the guard," Jeremiah said, his voice hardening with resolve. "You get inside and plant that charge. We can wait here in the support building until Kyano finds us."

"How sure are you that he will be here," Miranda asked, her voice laced with faint hints of doubt, "We don't even know if he will come today much less right to this exact spot!"

"If my hunch is right," replied Jeremiah, "Kyano will be back and even otherwise," he added, "We have to do something! We can't just lie in wait and hope that Hayada will not find us. What better place to hide than the one place she will not think to look for us at."

Miranda nodded, her hand already reaching for the door handle. "Be careful, Jeremiah," she said, her voice laced with concern.

Jeremiah smiled. "Always am."

The support building was a small single storied facility with no staff inside. It housed mainly interfaces that connected power, telephone and internet supply to the V5 campus. The grey and green building looked very nondescript with only one security guard standing in its front right corner. It had cameras on the side facing the main building but none towards the other side and hence the need for a guard who mostly patrolled the area that was out of view of the security camera.

Jeremiah made his way quickly to the front of the support building and jabbed the guard behind his neck, rendering him unconscious. Ensuring to stay out of sight of the security cameras, he dragged the guard into the building. He pulled out a screwdriver and covered his face with a black cloth. Sneaking under the cameras and making sure to stay out of sight, he undid the screws holding the cameras in place to move them away from their focal points, so they could do what they needed to do uninterrupted.

CHAPTER

23

Bright Shadows and Dark Light

The portal shimmered, a luminous tear in the fabric of reality, bridging the vibrant hues of Serinia with the muted tones of Earth. Kyano, Layana, and Merata stepped through, their senses adjusting to the shift in atmosphere, the subtle change in gravity, the unfamiliar weight of this mirrored world.

They stood in a secluded alleyway, the towering skyscrapers of the city casting long shadows that swallowed them whole. Kyano, his eyes scanning the surroundings, felt a surge of anticipation mixed with a grim determination. The time had come to confront Hayada, to challenge her reign of terror, to reclaim their stolen world.

"We need to blend in," Kyano said, his voice a low murmur that echoed in the confined space. "Earth clothes."

Merata nodded, "I don't suppose you have some lying around?" she inquired.

Kyano motioned to the clothing store close by and the three of them went in. Normally abuzz with tourists and regular shoppers, the store seemed a little empty that day. A quick glance at the clock on the wall let Kyano know that it was a weekday afternoon, and he deduced that to be a good reason for the lack of shoppers.

Kyano's knowledge of earth lent itself well to navigate the garments in the store that his companions were unfamiliar with. Not making any effort to be selective they chose their clothes and started to make their way to the till.

With a little twirl of his hand, Kyano manifested his wallet. One of the many things he stored in his inner sanctum when he left Earth to go back to Serinia. As they paid the bill, he noticed an earpiece worn by the salesperson at the till. He thought it odd that they were wearing it as they worked but then it hit him. It was a Vbuddy. Before he could tell the others to run for it, the store went dark and a wisp of black smoke emanated from behind one of the aisles and before they could fully react there were three Raka there, teeth bared and claws at the ready.

"Twin Magnus!" Layana called out her weapon and ducked underneath a swiping claw that came her way. The Raka slammed into the counter behind them and turned around quickly to run back at Layana. The warrior crouched and spun around with her blades bared in her outstretched arms. With a swift arc, she cut through the Raka, making it disappear. She then leapt up in the air and descended between the two remaining monsters, twirling around as she did, her blades making clean cuts at the Rakas' necks, rendering them both dead.

Kyano jumped across the counter as his sister battled the monsters and grabbed the earpiece from the salesperson. Throwing it at the ground he quickly stepped on it, breaking it in two.

"We have to go now!" he yelled, and a portal opened up in front of them and all three warriors ran through before more Raka could intercept them.

"How did she know we were here so quickly?" cried Merata as they stepped out of the portal and into yet another secluded alley, "We barely came out of the portal moments before the attack!"

"It's the little silver piece the person in the store was wearing on her ear, it's the earpiece I told you about," Kyano replied, "Hayada's Earth technology," he added, looking at Merata's searching expression, "It is what she is using to spread her gaze wider. Every person who is wearing one of those is Hayada's unwilling spy."

"There is no more time to waste!" retorted Layana, "Take us to Hayada right away and let's destroy her creation! If she has deployed her earpieces already, we cannot afford to lose another moment."

"We can't just waltz into V5 knowing what Hayada is capable of, can we?" retorted Kyano.

"What else do you think we should do then?" Layana questioned, surprised by her brother's tactics.

"If we ignore the fact that Hayada is a goddess who wants to destroy the universe, she is still one of the most powerful people on Earth," replied Kyano.

"We need to be tactful," he added, "Our one advantage right now is that there are more than seven billion people on Earth and not everyone has one of these things. So as powerful as Hayada is, she is not yet omnipresent. Our first step is to get in touch with Jeremiah and Miranda. Daryudan said they would have a plan and be ready to enact it once we arrived here. We need to find them and decipher what is happening but judging by the Raka that showed up to attack us moments after we appeared, Hayada has her eyes and ears spreading citywide and she might already know we are here. So, whatever we do, we need to avoid crowded places and avoid being seen by people. We have no idea who has an earpiece and who doesn't."

"We better find Jeremiah quickly then," replied Layana, "Chrytos!" she called forth her phoenix.

"Locate Jeremiah," she told him, "We need to speak with him at once!"

Chrytos, a fiery beacon against the gray cityscape, soared into the sky, his keen eyes scanning the urban landscape, his senses attuned to the faintest trace of Jeremiah's presence.

"He's close," Layana announced, her voice laced with a mix of relief and urgency. "Follow me."

They navigated the maze of streets, making sure to avoid main roads and sticking to alleys behind buildings and cutting through parks, their movements swift and purposeful, Chrytos circling overhead, guiding their path. They arrived at the car Miranda and Jeremiah used to reach V5.

"This is it," Chrytos declared, his eyes fixed on the vehicle. "Jeremiah's energy is very close but I cannot venture further without being seen by humans."

Kyano nodded, his hand instinctively clenching into a fist, "Wait here," he said, "I will call you when I find him."

"Our minds are connected," Chrytos said telepathically, "Go, Kyano," he added, "I will guide you the rest of the way."

Kyano donned the baseball cap he took from the clothing store and walked as quickly as he could, doing his best to blend in and not appear out of place. The strings of his hoodie dangled as he swiftly moved across the V5 campus trying to locate his uncle.

"Make a right turn," came Chrytos's voice, "You're close."

Kyano followed the silent instructions down to the dot.

"Stop!" came the next one and Kyano hid himself behind a car in the parking lot. "Move now," said Chrytos again, ushering Kyano on.

"He's in that structure ahead of you!" Chrytos finally said.

Kyano snuck into the support building and called out, "Miranda! Jeremiah!" making sure his voice was audible yet not loud.

"Over here," came Jeremiah's voice. He quickly glanced over at Miranda, "It is thrilling to be right for once!"

"You mean you had no idea he would come today?" asked a shocked Miranda.

"What does it matter now that he's here?" quipped Jeremiah.

Kyano jogged over and hugged his uncle and friend, "I found them," he told Chrytos mentally.

"Ok now what's the plan," he asked turning to Miranda.

"I have a makeshift EMP here," she told Kyano, "It will disrupt the internet for maybe twenty minutes at best and in that time, you need to attack Hayada with everything you've got. Kira has been downloaded into Hayada's mind and when she feels threatened, she will upload her code back into the V5 mainframe leaving Hayada vulnerable as the transfer happens. That is your best shot!"

"That is a much better plan than the one I had in mind," replied Kyano.

"Chrytos," he called, "Link Miranda and Jeremiah to us," he asked, "Layana! Merata! Hope you both are ready because it is time! I'll open a portal next to you both that will lead you to the lab. I will meet you there."

He then opened a portal for himself and turned to look at Miranda again, "You will hear me in your mind when I am in position!" he said and disappeared.

The air crackled with anticipation as Kyano, Layana, and Merata materialized in the research lab, their sudden appearance disrupting the eerie silence that had settled over the room.

Hayada, her eyes still closed, her consciousness now merged with Kira, searched the endless voices in her head as she sat at her desk in the penthouse office. The owner of the clothing store nearby had thought about strangely clothed people that came to her store, thought about how their clothes didn't seem like they were form a renaissance fair. Sensing these thoughts, Hayada sent Raka over to investigate and the Raka had not reported back which only meant that the warriors of light were now on Earth. It was only a matter of time before they reached V5 where she was confident that they would meet their demise.

As the warriors appeared, Kira was alerted to their presence, sensing the subtle changes in temperature emanating from the research lab. Although there were no cameras on that floor, there were other ways of detecting intrusions. Temperature sensors and pressure sensitive floors made sneaking into the lab very difficult without triggering the silent alarm that Kira would monitor. Even as Kyano and his companions made no efforts to conceal their presence, Hayada knew almost instantly when they appeared in her sanctuary of power.

"Intruders!" she hissed, her voice laced with a venomous fury. "You dare disrupt my ascension?" she said her thoughts aloud.

Her eyes snapped open, blazing with a cold fire, her form radiating a power that seemed to warp the very air around her. She rose from her chair and disappeared from her office in an instant. Darkness fell upon the lab with a sudden yet inevitable omen and Hayada was now face to face with the warriors of light.

"You will pay for your defiance," she snarled, her voice echoing through the lab, its walls trembling with her barely contained rage.

Kyano met her gaze, his expression unwavering, the Scythe of Serinia humming with a vibrant energy in his hand. "Hayada," he declared, his voice resonating with a steely determination, "your reign of terror ends now."

Hayada's eyes piqued at the sight of the weapon. She couldn't help but feel that she might have underestimated Kyano.

"So, my father favored you!" she snarled, "You will not leave here with your life or the Scythe!"

Layana and Merata, their weapons drawn, flanked Kyano, their faces etched with a fierce resolve. The lab, once a sterile sanctuary of technological innovation, had transformed into a battleground, the air thick with anticipation and the scent of impending conflict.

Hayada lunged forward, her form a blur of motion, her attack a whirlwind of dark energy aimed at Kyano's heart. He parried the blow, the Scythe's obsidian blade meeting her onslaught with a resounding clash that sent shockwaves rippling through the room.

The battle raged, a chaotic dance of light and shadow, of divine power and mortal defiance. Kyano, Layana, and Merata fought with a synchronized ferocity, their movements honed through countless battles, their weapons extensions of their will.

Hayada, her fury amplified by seeing the Scythe in Kyano's hands, the very weapon she once sought to steal in the mutinous act that led to her banishment, unleashed a torrent of attacks, her every strike infused with a destructive power that threatened to shatter the very foundations of the laboratory.

Kyano had to be smart about the way he battled. Their entire plan hinged on Kira downloading her code into the mainframe but if the battle raged on uncontrollably, he was afraid they would destroy the mainframe computer before the upload takes place. He parried Hayada's attacks, directing them away from the computer, the Scythe hummed in his hands as it absorbed the energy Hayada was attacking with and re-directing the fallout elsewhere. The walls of the lab on either side were the unfortunate victims and they began to crumble from the shockwaves released by the Scythe's redirections. Whatever he did,

Kyano had to make sure the mainframe computer set against the back wall was unharmed.

Raka started to pour into the cramped space and the warriors of light had to disband, their attentions diverted by the numerous intrusive monsters set to attack them.

"Just like the forest," Kyano said looking straight at Merata. She nodded and motioned to Layana to follow her, and they fell upon the Raka with precision and prejudice, cleaving, sheering, thrusting, stabbing and obliterating every monster that dared to stand in their way.

"Just you and me now," Kyano said, swirling the Scythe in his hand, his gaze fixed upon Hayada.

CHAPTER

24

The Responsibility of Pain

A maniacal laugh escaped her angry face as Hayada snapped her fingers. In moments, Kyano found himself facing the goddess of death in the netherworld. The landscape was a scorching mess of lava and brimstone, the air thick with smoke and despair. His eyes began to water but he held firm, his eyes transfixed on his ominous opponent. He couldn't help but feel a tinge of relief at the change of scenery, for now he could let loose and fight harder. There was no computer to protect.

"Getting uncomfortable, are we?" quipped the confident goddess, "Welcome to your doom!" and she was off in a flash. Swords, lances and spears emanated from out of nowhere within her grasp as she attacked Kyano with a speed that made Daryudan's attacks seem paltry. Kyano's Scythe, a whirlwind of obsidian fury, met Hayada's every assault, its blade deflecting her dark energy, its power a counterpoint to her chaotic might. His increased powers meant he had sharper senses now, the ability to see Hayada's attacks as they approached and fend them off.

"Fight me all you want, mortal" smirked Hayada, "I will alter your memories yet again and leave you here. You will be the first living mortal to be stuck in my prison for all eternity!" she sneered, "For your meddling, I will make sure you suffer a fate far worse than any other soul that is here."

"Why do you have to talk so much?" Kyano replied, knowing that his words would only enrage Hayada further, "Maybe fighting the Scythe is making you tired, you don't look like your divine self!" he taunted.

Kyano knew that he could not drag the battle on very long. He was still a mortal facing a goddess, Scythe or not, he would surely lose if the battle wore on. He had to get her back to the laboratory so Miranda could enact her plan and when Hayada was down, he would use the Scythe to end her life. The best way to do so was to enrage his opponent. To make her attack without precision, to expose any kinks in her attacks and take advantage when the opportunity presented itself.

The plan seemed to work so far as enraging Hayada was concerned. She attacked Kyano harder and faster, each attack stronger than the previous one, each weapon she conjured more potent than the last.

Hayada grew impatient as she watched Kyano fend off her attacks. She could tell that it took everything he had to keep fighting her but nonetheless, his defiance was frustrating her just the same as his words did. She threw a spear at him, and he sliced it in half with the Scythe. She roared, and a ball of flame the size of a dragon lunged out of her mouth and hurtled toward Kyano.

"Marailos!" he called, and his dragon came forth to meet the raging fireball with one of his own, cancelling it out.

Hayada conjured a monster, fashioned out of the fires of the netherworld itself, an undead dragon. The monster screeched, its high-pitched roar deafening and malicious. It took to the air and Marailos was off in the flash of a thunderclap. His claws met the beast's, and the monsters fought midair.

Putting her hands together, Hayada screamed. Pouring her black energy into a void, a portal she opened between her palms. Stretching her hand into it she pulled out a black sword, its blade glinting with avarice and its poisonous energy sent waves through the battlefield.

Kyano fought with every fiber of his being, parrying every slash, every thrust and cut. Hayada crouched low and swung high as he leapt out of the way, bringing the Scythe down below him to meet her rising blade. The weapons clashed in a thunderous stalemate as the ground below shook and cracked. The force of each attack ungodly, a fitting spectacle for the place beyond death. Blow after blow Kyano matched Hayada's attacks until she found an opening. She thrust her sword at his right shoulder to which he crouched, just in time for Hayada's well-aimed kick to catch him in the chest sending him flying into the air. He landed thirty feet away with a thud. Hayada was upon him in a flash, her hand stretched out and touched his face.

Memories of V5 and all that happened since the voicemail flashed in his mind as she feverishly tried to make him forget.

"It is over boy!" she laughed as Kyano screamed, writhing, resisting the intrusion on his mind. The world around him vanished and he appeared on a riverbank gasping for air. Hayada and the netherworld disappeared, and he could no longer feel the anguish he was going through mere moments ago.

"Careful now," said a voice and Kyano turned around. He could not believe his eyes. Before him, stood his mother. Smiling warmly at his surprised face she said, "Are you alright? You look like you've seen a ghost." She then smiled, as warmly as the sun that shone on him, his worries and doubts slowly started to fade.

"Come get some grub," came the voice of a man and Kyano looked up to see his father, King Kalius, only he was wearing a t shirt and flipping hot dogs at a barbeque. Overjoyed at the prospect of enjoying a meal with his family, Kyano jogged towards his parents. He sat down at the bench with them, his dog pawing at his leg to give him a bite to eat.

"Alright, alright," he said to the dog as he pinched off a piece of his hot dog and threw it affectionately towards his pet. To his surprise the dog did not eat the treat. He kept looking at Kyano. A longing, foreboding look in his eyes. Confused, Kyano stared into his pet's eyes, trying to decipher what was being conveyed to him.

A teardrop escaped his eye as realization dawned on him. The dog was not his pet. It was Marailos trying to wrench Kyano out of Hayada's spell. With one last look at the idyllic life he was being shown, tears streaming down his face freely now, he closed his eyes and focused. With all his might, he concentrated on his inner sanctum. The pain in his head returned with a vengeance and the illusion started to crumble. The park and river disappeared, and his parents withered into dust. The world around him quaked and crumbled and he found himself sprawled on the floor of his inner sanctum.

The Scythe that he still held in his hand hummed and throbbed, pleading with him to act against the attack. He watched as Hayada's black energy attempted to shroud his green orb and he knew he had to do something before it was too late.

With every ounce of will in his being he pushed himself. "You will not have my mind!" he screeched, every word punctuated with his struggle to free himself of Hayada's influence.

He muscled himself into action and swung the Scythe at the encroaching black malice, severing its influence.

Hayada reeled, shocked at the event that just transpired, her body thrust into the air as if kicked by a giant, she fell to the ground a few feet away.

There was no time to lose. Now was Kyano's chance. He got to his feet trembling, still shaking from the effects of Hayada's attack. Seeing that he was the first to his feet he took his chance. He ran toward Hayada as swiftly as his legs would carry him. With the Scythe raised he opened a portal underneath her and swung with all his might. Hayada lifted her blade to block him but the force of Kyano's attack was too strong and having a portal under feet meant there was no footing to gain hold of. Hayada and Kyano hurtled into the black void as Marailos disappeared in the sky above them.

Layana's Twin Magnus, a symphony of golden blades, danced around the Raka, their sharp edges slicing through the monsters' hides, their swift movements creating a mesmerizing spectacle of deadly grace.

Merata, her movements a blur of deadly precision, weaved through the chaos, her sword and dagger finding their marks with pinpoint accuracy, drawing blood, inflicting pain, destroying every Raka she touched with her assassin's blade, Assylia.

The lab echoed with the clash of weapons, the hiss of energy, the cries of defiance, and the snarls of frustration. The battle raged, a desperate struggle for survival, a clash of wills that would determine the fate of worlds.

Kyano's portal opened on the ceiling and Hayada landed with a thud.

"Now!" rang Kyano's voice in Miranda's mind and she flipped the switch. The EMP whirred to life and with a few sparks and ensuing clicks, the support building shut down. Miranda quickly moved over to the back up switch and flicked it down to the off position.

Back in the lab, the lights went dark and the yellow emergency beacons turned on. Alarms blazed as the P.A system came to life again, "Internet access interrupted," said Kira's voice, "Switching to emergency power to enact project stockpile." This was the time.

Kyano raised his Scythe and with all his might he swung at Hayada, screaming with all the pain she put him through, aimed at her shoulder. She raised her sword to meet his, but he would not relent. A stalemate to decide the fate of the world ensued in the next moments. Kyano wrenched his hands, pouring his green energy to bolster his attack as he pushed down on the goddess of darkness. Merata and Layana joined him, lending their own power to the attack and the warriors of light pushed, with all their might and energy, they pushed.

Cracks began to appear on Hayada's sword and her eyes darted. The grimace of malice she had was now replaced with a most unfamiliar feeling. Fear. The relentless attack broke through the sword and the Scythe of Serinia drew Hayada's blood as it crashed into her left shoulder.

She screamed from the pain, reeling under the force of the attack. Kyano pushed the weapon lower into her shoulder, all the way through her collar bone and stopped just before he sliced through her heart.

In Hayada's mind the rash of multicolored lights that flew across the sky abruptly stopped and changed course away from her. They now flowed backwards away from where she stood.

"Wait, stop!" she cried but to no avail.

"Failsafe protection protocol now in effect," came Kira's robotic voice, "Transferring consciousness code to mainframe!"

Hayada squealed in pain as her mind was ravaged by Kira.

The eerie silence in the support building had an air of confidence brewing within. A victorious smile started to spread on Miranda's face, which had been stern until her EMP charge worked.

"There is one other possibility," Miranda said to Jeremiah, "In theory of course."

"And what might that be?" he asked, as he waited impatiently to hear Kyano's voice again before the power came back on. He couldn't help but notice Miranda's smile, "Share the secret," he egged her on, "Judging by that smile it has to be something good."

"If Kira merged with Hayada's consciousness, when the failsafe protocol goes into effect," she trailed off..

"Well," nudged Jeremiah.

"It might, in theory, pull Hayada's consciousness out of her body as well and into the mainframe." She replied.

Hayda wrenched her back and screamed in pain as her mind split itself.

"Not like this!" he roared, "I cannot die!" Her screams were deafening and yet Kyano could only think of one thing to say in response.

"On behalf of Serinia and Earth, goodbye and farewell." He pulled the Scythe free of her shoulder and watched as her consciousness separated from her body making the goddess write and twist in unimaginable pain. Watching the spectacle, he fought so hard to realize, empathy crept into his mind and perhaps softened his heart a little to the plight of another's suffering. He wondered if this was revenge or justice. Such was the responsibility the warriors of light were meant to bear. The responsibility of pain.

Hayada realized in horror as the out of body experience she was beginning to feel only deepened. Her mind form lifted off the ground of her own inner sanctum and got pulled away with the flickering lights in the sky toward a white dot on the distant horizon. Hayada's consciousness along with Kira had left her body and was now in the mainframe computer.

Kyano raised the Scythe and thought of all the torture, all the pain and suffering inflicted by a selfish megalomaniacal goddess who couldn't understand the simple truth of live and let live.

With prejudice and anger coursing through his very being he struck the main frame computer making it explode. Hayada's lifeless body lay on the ground behind him. The power came back on, and the halide system took effect, blasting the lab with inert gases to put out the fire emanating from the computer. Holding their breath, Kyano, Merata and Layana coughed as the intrusive air did its job and began extinguishing the flames of their victory.

The Raka that remained ran for their lives unaware that Chrytos the ever-vigilant beast of lore, awaited their exit. The phoenix killed every one of them, his wings slicing through their bodies like they were made of butter. The warriors of light left the research lab and ran down the corridor to the elevator entrance. They slumped down to the floor, now that they were free of the halide system's unbreathable air.

"We have to go," said Kyano, "We don't want to be seen by anyone."

"Can we just take a moment to celebrate what we accomplished," Merata replied, gasping for breath, unable to hold herself from smiling.

Smiling back at her, Kyano took to a jog. He could have opened a portal, but he felt like running. For the first time in a long time, he truly felt free. Their victory meant freedom, not just to them but to everyone on Serinia and Earth and he relished that thought. Screams of joy erupted from all three of them as their jog turned into a sprint and they ran. They ran through the building and to the support structure where Miranda and Jeremiah awaited them. Kyano waved the Scythe as they reached their companions and opened a portal to Laira.

"We won!" he screamed as he hugged his uncle. Layana and Merata joined in and so did Miranda. Their huddle interrupted by the sirens of approaching emergency vehicles, their smiles unwavering and their minds feeling an ease that seemed lost forever, the friends stepped through the portal to go back to Serinia.

As they left, Miranda could not help but wonder what the magical world was like. She hoped she would fit in well and make new friends.

Kyano's mind could only focus on relief. They had won. They crafted a risky plan and executed it to perfection. They defeated Hayada. The goddess of death herself. They trapped her consciousness in a machine and destroyed it. The irony of human technology, of human life itself crept into his mind. *We are our own worst enemy* rang his old teacher's voice in his mind and, in that moment, Kyano truly felt that it was apt. Technology, meant for the betterment of society, was what helped them win in the end. It was not the Scythe; it was not the king of gods and his unlimited power, and it was not magic. It was technology. A power that was man made. It was only fitting that mankind rose against an oppressive goddess to put an end to her tyranny.

EPILOGUE

Part One: Joy of Victory, Year of Peace

The sun shone brightly upon the city of Laira, casting a golden glow upon the bustling crowds that thronged the streets. A sense of joyous anticipation hung in the air, a palpable wave of relief and excitement rippling through the city's inhabitants.

The massive oak gates swung open, revealing five figures striding purposefully towards the city center. Kyano, Layana, and Merata, their faces etched with a mix of triumph and weariness, led the way, their battle-worn armor gleaming in the sunlight. Behind them, Jeremiah and Miranda, their expressions a mix of awe and determination, followed closely, their eyes wide with wonder at the sights and sounds of this fantastical world.

As far as the citizens could see, they were attacked by dark creatures and the warriors of light vanquished them. Daryudan kept true to his word and retreated, Raka began to make their way back from human lands, back to where their lord summoned them, back to the dark lands.

News such as that was hard to contain and word of Raka retreating to the dark lands had spread like wildfire. Lairans waited with bated breaths to welcome their triumphant heroes and when they saw them return, when they saw the smile on the face of their Queen, they knew. They knew that the warriors of light were victorious. Cheers erupted; a thunderous wave of jubilation echoed through the city streets.

Layana, her voice amplified by the joyous clamor, addressed her people, her words carrying a weight of authority and heartfelt gratitude. They made their way to the palace steps and the crowd followed them. The glee and relief in the faces of the warriors only spread through the gathering crowd and by the time they reached the palace, the whole city was there, waiting to hear from their Queen.

As they reached the ornate marble steps, Layana spun around. She surveyed the crowd that gathered, her own honor guard led by Saldah, stood at the foot of the magnificent staircase, an ever-present vigil, a symbol of the Queen's strength.

"People of Laira," she proclaimed, her voice ringing with a triumphant clarity, "we have returned. And we bring with us news that will forever change the course of our history."

She paused, her gaze sweeping across the eager faces before her. "Hayada, the goddess of chaos, the architect of our suffering, is no more."

A collective gasp of disbelief rippled through the crowd, followed by wave after wave of joyous cheers and unrestrained celebration.

Layana raised her hand high in the air and screamed in joy with her citizens, "We *WON!*"

As the sun began to set, casting a warm glow upon the jubilant city, a sense of peace and unity settled over Laira. The warriors of light, their mission fulfilled, their bond strengthened by the trials they had endured, stood together, their gazes fixed upon the horizon, their hearts filled with hope for a brighter future.

The war was over. The darkness had been vanquished. And Serinia, bathed in the warm light of a new dawn, was finally free.

"And now," Layana declared, "There is one final thing left to do." She turned to Kyano and motioned him to the front.

"The kingdom of Serin had fallen at the hands of the dark army," she announced, "As you are all aware, this left a huge gash in our hearts.

One that could not be filled simply by vengeance. And so, today, I announce that Laira will help rebuild this beacon of hope, to rebuild the kingdom that was the spearhead in the war that lasted sixty generations. To rebuild the kingdom of Serin which will be helmed by its true king."

She took a knee, and the crowd followed, "Welcome!" she declared, "to the reign of King Kyano Thrinio!"

The crowd erupted with deafening cheers. The jubilation that reverberated through the entire city was a clear indicator of the love and affection the people had toward Layana and Kyano.

"Your highness!" acknowledged Merata and Kyano nodded to her.

He raised his hand up for all to see, the Scythe of Serinia held high. A symbol of victory, a symbol of hope and the usher of peace that would follow until he had to battle Daryudan again. He had one year and then he would have to keep his promise. A promise he made to the most hated foe in all Serinia. Fate, it seemed, was not without its share of irony. Daryudan played a subtle yet pivotal role in the fall of Hayada and Kyano could only hope that when the year was over, he could settle his differences with Daryudan without needless bloodshed.

Part Two: The coils of the Serpent of Death

The air in the lab at V5 still crackled with the fading remnants of the battle, a sharp acrid odor from the halon fire extinguisher and the smell of burnt metal still lingered like a ghost. Daryudan stepped through the shimmering portal, his eyes immediately drawn to Hayada's lifeless form sprawled on the floor. A triumphant grin spread across his face, and a harsh laugh erupted from his throat, echoing through the silent laboratory.

"Well, well, well," he sneered, his voice dripping with sardonic amusement. "Behold; the fruit of betrayal!"

He sauntered towards Hayada's unmoving form, his heavy boots crunching on the debris scattered across the floor. He knelt beside her, his gaze tracing the lines of her pale face, the vacant stare of her lifeless eyes.

"Not so mighty now, are you, goddess?" he taunted, his voice laced with bitter satisfaction. "Your grand plans, your dreams of omnipotence... all reduced to ashes."

He chuckled, a low rumble that vibrated through the room. "Did you truly believe you could control me, Hayada? Did you think I would be your pawn in this little game of yours?" he sneered, his expression quickly changing from glee to serious resentment, "I, who loathes betrayal above all else? When you came to free me from the netherworld, I hatched my plan. I decided the moment I laid eyes on you, that I would cause your demise and look!" he declared, "It is I who stands victorious over your dead body."

He leaned closer, his voice dropping to a conspiratorial whisper. "I manipulated you, Hayada. I planted the seeds of your destruction, nurtured them with subtle suggestions, and watched with amusement as you danced to my tune."

He gestured towards the shattered remains of the mainframe computer, a twisted smile playing on his lips. "I led the warriors of light to your doorstep, Hayada. I orchestrated your downfall." Yet another maniacal laugh escaped Daryudan's jubilant form, "It was I, who told that Hawthorne woman about your desire for being everywhere, knowing everything."

"I was specific, Hayada," he said, his voice a low growl. "I spoke of merging consciousness, not power. And she listened. She heard exactly what I needed her to hear."

He stood up, his gaze fixed on Hayada's lifeless form. "How does it feel, goddess?" he asked, his voice laced with a cruel mockery. "To be betrayed by the very creature you sought to control?"

He raised his hand, and the obsidian Halberd materialized in his grasp, its blade humming with a dark energy. He plunged the Halberd into Hayada's chest, a surge of power flowing from her lifeless body into his own.

"Your power is mine now, Hayada," he declared, his voice resonating with a newfound strength. "And I will use it to reshape this world, to create a new order, wherein darkness reigns supreme."

He withdrew the Halberd, its blade now pulsating with Hayada's stolen power. His undead form began to morph back to color. The pallor and gashes on his face and neck healing to reveal the hues he had in life. He cast one last glance at her lifeless form, his eyes gleaming with a triumphant fire.

"After all this time Hayada," he said to her, "You held up your end of the bargain. You gave me a weapon that could rival the Scythe. And I will use it to bring forth a reality that will end the madness of creation and death. I will realize your dream and sit atop your throne and mock you for eternity. That is what you deserve. That is what your betrayal was worth."

With a final, sardonic laugh, he turned and strode towards the portal, his form disappearing into the swirling vortex, leaving behind the shattered remnants of Hayada's reign and the chilling promise of a new era of darkness.

In the chaos of simmering smoke and blaring alarms, the laboratory started to quiet down, the bustle of battle ended leaving behind the telltale wreckage of an uncontrolled fight. Amidst the carnage that ended a reign of terror, sat the broken hard drive of the mainframe. A small, arhythmic blink of its yellow LED a promise of undying hate and determination.

THANK YOU, DEAR READER

When I finished writing volume 3, I was at a loss of how to progress the story forward. The only thing I knew in my heart then was that this was a powerful story. It had immense potential to be a great one and I hesitated. For five years, I hesitated for I did not know what the best path forward was. I could not bring myself to put pen to paper until I was absolutely certain that the path I choose to take the story forward on was the path my work was meant to take. I determined to make this book the best one in the series so far and worked to realize that goal. Thank you so much for reading my work for without you and your penchant for reveling in my dreams, I could not have dreamt this novel.

Until next time,
Kartik